W9-BRH-917

DOLLS *of* WAR

DOLLS
of
WAR

SHIRLEY PARENTEAU

CANDLEWICK PRESS

First edition 2017

Library of Congress Catalog Card Number pending
ISBN 978-0-7636-9069-4

17 18 19 20 21 22 BVG 10 9 8 7 6 5 4 3 2 1

Printed in Berryville, VA, U.S.A.

This book was typeset in Walbaum.

Candlewick Press
99 Dover Street
Somerville, Massachusetts 02144

visit us at www.candlewick.com

— *For Bill, always* —

CHAPTER 1

Stanby, Oregon
August 14, 1941

Macy James tightened her hands over the back of her mother's wheeled chair while she tried to send silent "be quiet" messages toward her friend Lily. She glanced at a tall Japanese girl doll on a stand nearby, trying to absorb Miss Tokyo's calm. She glanced at the doll several times, because what she really wanted to do was shove Lily through the Stanby Museum's tall front doors and lock them after her.

Lily wasn't looking at Macy, so she didn't see the warning Macy was sending. Lily was looking at Mama. Once, Mama's hair had been as thick as Macy's and an even sunnier brown. Lily was seeing thinning blond. She was seeing Mama's sharp cheekbones and the fragile shape of her arms and legs and she was being honest again.

"They have earthquakes in Japan," Lily said in her best know-it-all voice. "We learned about them in geography. Remember, Macy?"

"Of course I remember. And so does Mama. She *lived* there when she was ten like us. Her father worked for the American ambassador. Didn't he, Mama?"

Her mother smiled gently. She no longer had the energy for a lively discussion. Again, Macy wanted to shove Lily outside.

Lily still wasn't seeing the message. "And they have volcanoes!" she went on. "And hilly streets. Those streets would be hard for you, Mrs. James. You probably couldn't get up them in your chair."

Lily's mother called honesty a virtue and said that people should face the truth. *What I think,* Macy told herself, *is that making someone face the truth can sometimes just be a way of making them feel bad.*

"Besides," Lily added, still being honest, "that Japanese doll has been on display forever. You should put it in storage and set out something new for people to see."

Mama started to answer but broke into one of her bouts of coughing. Shaking her head in apology, she pushed the chair's wheels to roll backward, away from them.

Macy took the opportunity to hiss at Lily. "You *know* Mama loves Miss Tokyo. And she loves Japan. That's why she carries that big book filled with pictures from there. How can you be so mean?"

"Mean?" Lily's brown eyes got wider. "When was I being mean?"

"When you said she shouldn't travel to Japan, that's when."

"Well, she shouldn't, Macy. You moved to Stanby two years ago because she couldn't take the damp weather at the coast. Listen to her coughing now. Do you think she's strong enough for a trip to Japan?"

"She wants to meet the artist who created Miss Tokyo." Macy turned toward the doll. Miss Tokyo was meant to look like a ten-year-old girl. On her foot-high floor stand, she stood almost as tall as Macy. "I'm not going to tell Mama she can't travel. Neither is Papa. She needs to believe she can."

"But Macy—"

"When we came here," Macy said, cutting into

Lily's protest, "Miss Tokyo was in a back room with her little dishes and lamps and things scattered around. Nick helped Mama get them all together and Mama arranged every one of them. She *earned* the trip."

"Where is Nick?" Lily glanced around.

"He's somewhere with his friend Hap. Getting older," Macy said, almost as amused as her seventeen-year-old brother by Lily's crush.

As Lily made a face at the reminder of the difference in age, Mama rolled forward again. Macy darted over to help position her beside Miss Tokyo. The big book filled with colored pictures of Japan was starting to slip from her lap. Macy straightened it before pressing Mama's shoulder in sympathy for the coughing. Inside, she worried.

Everyone could see that Mama was growing weaker. To hide the thoughts that might be showing on her face, Macy looked again at the doll. Gleaming black hair framed Miss Tokyo's dark moveable eyes and gentle almost-smile.

Her heavy blue silk kimono glowed. Papa always pointed out to museum visitors that the hand-painted peach blossoms on the silk were a design chosen for the doll by the empress's own dressmaker.

= 4 =

Almost every day, Macy and Mama pretended to discuss the flowers and temples in the pictures in Mama's book with Miss Tokyo. And every day, they planned a trip to Japan they would make together.

Papa had said privately that Mama might never again be strong enough to travel, but he pretended, the way Macy did. Sometimes, Macy wondered if Mama was pretending, too.

And here was Lily, being honest and ruining it all.

This time, she caught Macy's glare. Her cheeks turning red, she said, "My mama's expecting me home," and ran out.

As the solid doors of the Stanby Museum thudded shut, Mama drew Macy closer to her chair. Her eyes no longer danced with her love for life as they had even last fall, but they were still the same clear green as Macy's. "Lily feels left out, sweetheart. We won't speak of Japan in front of her again. It would not be kind."

Lily's not being kind, Macy thought, but she said only, "When you feel better, you'll show me Miss Tokyo's country the way you saw it years ago. We'll have so much fun!"

"Of course we will." Mama's eyes glittered. "I look forward to our trip more than anything.

You will love the kind people I knew as a child."
Raising her hands to her neck, she removed a chain
she always wore.

A tiny *kokeshi* doll hung from the fine gold
links. The cylindrical doll with a ball-shaped head
and no arms or legs was even smaller than one of
Miss Tokyo's fingers.

"Your little doll is so cute," Macy said softly.
"It must have been exciting to meet the doll maker
who made it. He was the father of the artist who
made Miss Tokyo?"

"Yes. Gouyou the first, as he's known now. He
was celebrated as an artist who created lifelike
dolls. Miss Tokyo was created by his son and always
makes me think of him. You can see the artist's
kindness in the loving way he shaped and painted
the doll."

Macy imagined the artist's hands as he followed
the natural curve of Miss Tokyo's cheeks with his
chisel. "Did he have a model or did he carve her
from memory?"

"The artist I met didn't create Miss Tokyo,"
Mama reminded her, her voice wistful. "He was
training his young son when I knew him. The son,
Hirata Gouyou the second, later became a master

doll artist, too. It was he who carved and painted our Miss Tokyo."

"*Ikiningyo.*" Macy rolled the Japanese word on her tongue, remembering that *ningyo* meant "doll" and that *iki* meant "lifelike."

"Both doll makers, father and son, gained wide admiration for their *ikiningyo.*" Mama's voice warmed with memory, as it always did. "I was no older than you when I visited Gouyou-san's studio." She turned the tiny doll in her hand. "When we had admired the beautiful lifelike dolls, the artist gave me this little *kokeshi* to take home with me."

"But she didn't have a hole in her hair then," Macy said, enjoying Mama's pleasure in reliving a time when she had been so happy.

"When we returned to America," Mama said, her voice sounding stronger as she relaxed into the memory, "my father paid a jeweler to drill a hole through the little painted topknot. He threaded a gold chain through so I could wear it."

Her hands trembled as she held the chain toward Macy. "I want you to wear it now."

Macy bent forward because Mama was waiting, but inside, she felt alarm she didn't understand. "But Mama, you always wear it."

"And now you will." Mama settled the tiny doll at Macy's collar. "The little *kokeshi* looks sweet on you. Don't you agree, Miss Tokyo?"

She waited expectantly while Macy tried to hide a growing ache in her heart.

Nearly every day since Papa became curator of the museum, she and Mama had pretended to pick up the tiny cups to sip tea with the doll. They talked with Miss Tokyo and took turns answering for her.

Now Mama was waiting for her to say, in the high-pitched voice they gave the doll, "Yes, Mama-san, she looks very nice."

But fear for her mother grew stronger, and she could only say, "I'll take good care of her. And I'll watch over Miss Tokyo. I'll watch over them both forever!"

CHAPTER 2

December 8, 1941

Macy looked away as Lily raised an imaginary machine gun toward imaginary Japanese warplanes flying over the American flag hanging in the school yard, screaming firing sounds. "Akk! Akk! Akk!"

Everyone in the country hates Japan today, Macy thought. *Everyone but me, and I don't know how to feel.*

Betsy Oshima, a fourth-grader, ran by using one hand to hold her other arm high as she aimed at imaginary planes. "Pow! Pow! I got one! Pow!"

One of Macy's fifth-grade classmates shoved red hair back from his eyes and looked at Betsy in disgust. "You're shooting your own people."

"I'm shooting our enemy, Mark. The way you are."

"Japs are the enemy. You're a Jap."

Did that mean Betsy was the enemy? Macy wanted to say something but wasn't sure what. Betsy was fun. Everyone liked her. It wasn't fair to blame her for Pearl Harbor.

As Macy groped for words, Betsy shook her head, making her black hair fly. "Uh-uh. I was born here. My parents were born here. We're Americans, just like you."

She raised her arm again and ran toward her friends from the fourth grade. "Akk! Akk! Akk! There goes another one!"

"Jerk!" Macy exclaimed to Mark.

Whether Betsy's words made any difference to Mark was hard to tell. But he found a new argument to answer Macy. "Girls don't shoot down planes."

Now Lily was offended. "Why not?"

"Because you're girls." Mark ran off to join friends, all of them boys aiming pretend guns toward the sky.

"That's not a reason!" Macy shouted, raising her own pretend gun.

Lily's anger vanished in a laugh. "It's a reason to boys." She stopped laughing and looked more closely at Macy. "You look kind of white. Are you worried about Miss Tokyo?"

Macy dropped her imaginary machine gun, her arm falling to her side. Mama had loved the big Japanese doll right up to her death, three months ago. Yesterday's awful news on the radio had made Macy feel like taffy on a hook pulled in two directions. She loved the doll more than anything. She felt as if the doll captured part of Mama. But disease had killed Mama. Now Japanese bombers had killed American sailors. And people like Mark were blaming the deaths at Pearl Harbor on everyone and maybe everything that looked Japanese.

"She's just a doll," she said to Lily. "Betsy Oshima didn't have anything to do with bombing Pearl Harbor. And neither did Miss Tokyo." *If anything happens to Mama's doll . . .* She couldn't finish the thought.

"She came from our enemy," Lily warned. "Remember, the museum is named for Professor

Stanby, like the town. The museum and everything in it represent the town. Nobody wants an enemy doll to represent them!"

Macy didn't want to talk about Miss Tokyo. She didn't want to remind anyone of the doll in the museum. Instead, she said, "The Japanese bombed our ships on a Sunday. A Sunday!"

Lily agreed with a shiver. "I'm not sure how far away Pearl Harbor is, but it's in Hawaii, and the Hawaiian Islands are in our own Pacific Ocean!" Her eyes got wider. "Those planes *might* come here!"

Would they? Could they fly so far? "Papa says the world will never go back to the way things were before the bombing."

Papa had made it sound like change might be a good thing, as if a new path might help them stop hearing Mama's voice and feeling her touch every time they turned around. Macy clutched the small *kokeshi* doll she had worn on its chain since the day Mama put it around her neck. *How can I hate the Japanese when Mama loved them?*

That same question had torn through her yesterday while she hovered near the radio with Nick and Papa, trying to understand the terrible news the reporters read in tight, angry voices. "Our navy was prepared," one broadcaster exclaimed. "Navy aircraft guns blazed, shooting down the attacking planes."

"What happened to all our ships based at Pearl Harbor?" Nick demanded.

The news broadcast switched from one to another reporter around the world, all saying pretty much the same thing. "That's all they're allowed to tell us," Papa said. "The Japanese have attacked Pearl Harbor from the air."

"But what's the damage to all our ships at Pearl?" Nick demanded again.

Papa leaned back from the radio, straightening his shoulders. "Reporters have to watch their words. The government doesn't want the Japanese to learn how much damage has been done."

"They'll know. Their pilots will report it." Frustration shook Nick's voice. "They can't miss the sinking ships or sailors trying to swim through water blazing with burning oil."

Macy couldn't stop a choked gasp.

Papa glanced at her and motioned Nick to silence. "We'll know the facts in good time, son. We know all we need to know right now."

"I know all *I* need to know," Nick said with a resolve that scared Macy all over again. A reporter had just declared, "All recruiting stations will be open tomorrow at eight a.m."

Nick was only seventeen, too young to sign up, she assured herself, and she kept listening to the radio for facts the announcers weren't able to provide.

Those planes had done terrible damage. Macy knew it as well as Nick and Papa, whatever the radio people held back. The truth was in their hard voices, if not in their careful reporting.

The kids pretending to shoot down planes this morning knew it, too. Screams for revenge ripped through the school yard. "Remember Pearl Harbor!"

"They caught our boys sleeping! We're all awake now!"

"Here comes another rotten Zero! Shoot 'im, boys!"

Nearly everyone in the school yard raised imaginary guns to shoot down the imaginary Japanese plane with red circles on its body and wings. As Macy watched, she felt a shiver of fear. She couldn't think of a way to help Betsy Oshima. But maybe Papa should put Miss Tokyo into storage.

Moments later, Lily grabbed her arm. "Don't look! Look! No, don't look! Christopher Adams is coming over! He's going to talk to us!"

"You don't have to shriek." Macy sounded

sharper than she meant to and gave her friend a weak smile of apology. Last week, she'd have been more than happy if Christopher talked to her. He was smart and funny and collected popular girls as fast as their teacher caught whispers. Christopher didn't care. He laughed away flirty smiles and fluttery eyelashes.

He was probably the only boy in school who didn't follow after Rachel Rivers, the flirtiest of them all.

He wasn't laughing now. His mouth was in a hard line. When he stopped in front of Macy, dangerous sparks in his blue eyes made her take a step back. "Someone said you have a giant Japanese doll in your living room. Is that true?"

"She isn't in our living room. She's in the Stanby Museum. My dad runs it, and we live next door." Macy stepped forward again, challenging him. "So what? She's just a doll."

Miss Tokyo was a lot more than just a doll, but Christopher didn't need to know all of it. He wouldn't listen anyway, with his eyes flashing like he wanted to fight somebody.

"The people who made her killed our sailors," he said. "If you like stuff they made, you like them! That makes you a traitor."

Stung, Macy exclaimed, "I don't like war!"

"Then make your dad get rid of the doll."

"He can't get rid of her. She belongs to the museum." As if she *could* make Papa do anything. He hardly even talked to her since they lost Mama.

"Then *we'll* get rid of it," Christopher said. "I'll get my dad to take some men over there."

"No!" The word leaped from Macy. "She's just a doll," she said again.

"If you don't get rid of it, you're a rotten traitor," Christopher said. "And so is your father."

He might as well have said, *And so was your mother, for loving that doll, for loving all things Japanese.*

Anger raged through anguish. Macy knew she would always stick up for Mama's doll, even against Christopher Adams. As he turned to walk away, she grabbed for his shoulder. "Take that back!"

He swung around faster than she expected, but tripped and landed hard on his rear. The look of disbelief on his face made Macy bite back a laugh. Christopher Adams was too perfect to be sitting in the dirt at her feet.

His shock quickly turned thunderous. "She shoved me. You all saw that! She attacked when my back was turned. Just like those sneaky Japs she loves so much!"

He leaped to his feet and grabbed the *kokeshi* doll on its chain around her neck. He yanked. The chain snapped.

"Stop!" she screamed.

The broken links burned across her skin.

"This is Jap stuff," he yelled, waving the tiny doll. "What do we do with Jap stuff?"

"Stomp it!" someone shouted.

Christopher flung it onto the walk. Mark slammed one shoe down, snapping the round head from the cylinder-shaped body.

Macy lunged for the doll pieces. Miss Lawrence, one of the teachers, caught her as she snatched them from the pavement. The teacher grabbed Christopher with her free hand. Her eyes narrowed behind round glasses. "What is going on here?"

Fury boiled through Macy, making it hard to put the right words together. "He broke my necklace. And my doll. And he called my mother a traitor."

"What!" Christopher yelped. "I didn't say anything about your mother."

"Inside," Miss Lawrence ordered. "Both of you. You can talk this over with Principal Bates."

Macy's whole body had burned with anger, but now she felt cold. She had never been sent to the principal's office. She pictured it as some sort of dungeon: dark, with spears on the walls and a paddle in a desk drawer. No one was sent there unless they did something terrible.

She looked at the teacher. "I don't need to see the principal. I'll never talk to Christopher again."

"And I'll never talk to her," Christopher muttered. He grabbed the broken chain and hurled it toward her.

Miss Lawrence waited for Macy to shove the chain and broken *kokeshi* into a pocket, then marched them both toward the office. There was no choice but to hurry along with her into the school and down the hall.

"Wait here," Miss Lawrence said. "One against this wall, the other over there."

Christopher crossed his arms over his chest, his body looking rigid as he leaned against the nearest wall. He didn't even bother to push his dark-blond hair away from his eyes. It had a habit of falling over his forehead. Today, he didn't seem to care.

She had never liked Mark, but how had she ever liked Christopher? She wouldn't make that mistake again.

Macy crossed to the far side of the hall. She

stared at the floor to avoid looking at Christopher while Miss Lawrence went into the principal's office and closed the door.

I couldn't just walk away, she told herself. *Not after he grabbed Mama's* kokeshi *doll. What is Papa going to say? Principal Bates is sure to call him.*

The principal would call Christopher's parents, too. The thought made her look at him, after all, wondering what he was thinking.

He glared straight at her, finally pushing his hair out of his eyes. "Traitor!"

She caught her breath. "Take that back!"

The principal's door opened. "Mr. Bates is ready for you," Miss Lawrence told them. Her low-heeled shoes tap-tapped a warning against the wood floor as she walked away.

CHAPTER 3

What if they didn't go in? The teacher wasn't watching. But they both knew they didn't have a choice. Miss Nicholson, the school secretary, was already beckoning them inside. Macy walked toward her and heard Christopher follow.

Ahead lay the principal's office, where bad kids were sent.

"I don't belong here," Macy told Miss Nicholson. "I didn't do anything wrong."

Behind her, Christopher jeered. "Ha!"

The secretary simply pointed toward a second doorway to the right. It took all the courage Macy could find to walk through. No weapons threatened from the walls. A picture of a smiling President Roosevelt hung near the principal's desk, with a picture of George Washington nearby.

Principal Bates was a big man who sat behind a bigger-than-normal desk that should have been doomsday black instead of paneled with a warm wood. He studied them across steepled fingers before speaking in a calm voice, not at all like the scolding Macy had been bracing to hear. "What brings the two of you to see me?"

"You have a traitor in your school, sir," Christopher announced.

Heat rushed back into Macy's face. "He's mad because of the Japanese doll in our museum, the *Friendship* Doll."

"A real American would burn anything from Japan," Christopher said. "Especially a doll that looks like one of them. She says she won't. So she's a traitor. Isn't she?"

Macy twisted her hands together to keep from accidentally on purpose twisting them in his hair. "Miss Tokyo belongs to the museum."

"Friendship Doll," Principal Bates repeated. "I've seen her: a doll the size of a small girl."

The lecture she often heard Papa give visitors

burst from Macy. "They're sometimes called Dolls of Gratitude. Japanese children"—she glanced at Christopher—"who wanted to be *friends* sent Miss Tokyo and fifty-seven other dolls like her to America. They were to thank American children for sending thousands of smaller dolls to them way back in 1927, before I was even born."

The principal leaned back in his chair. "Fourteen years ago, yes. Two of our classes saved money to send a doll with the others. A cakewalk brought in enough to buy the steamship ticket. All the dolls carried steamship tickets along with passports and visas, as if they were living children. Everyone hoped the project would create such warm friendship that the two countries would never fight each other."

Macy risked a *So there* look at Christopher, but he wasn't looking at her. He was staring at Principal Bates as if he'd uncovered another traitor. She said a little louder than necessary, "American children sent almost thirteen thousand *Friendship Dolls* to children in Japan."

"A good number of dolls, an amazing number," the principal mused aloud. "I remember that children in nearly every one of the forty-eight states took part."

"We're at war *now*," Christopher pointed out. "The Japs bombed us. It didn't work."

"America is sure to join the war as soon as Congress can vote. Tragically, the dream of friendship failed." The principal gazed at Macy. "How many big Japanese dolls did you say were sent to thank the children here?"

"Fifty-eight," Macy said. She clasped the *kokeshi* doll in her pocket. "The finest doll artists in Japan competed for the right to make them. We're *lucky* to have one in our museum." She glared so hard at Christopher he should have felt her eyes burning holes in his head.

"Pearl Harbor," Christopher said to Principal Bates, as if those two words could make the doll project meaningless. His face reddened and he added with sudden anguish, "My uncle Ray is there. . . . We don't know if he's . . . if he's . . . We don't know yet."

Macy's anger faded. She wanted to offer sympathy but knew he wouldn't want that, not from her. Not now.

"We all feel the pain of the attack," Principal Bates assured him.

"Pain?" Christopher's voice rose. "Those sneaking

cowards sank our ships. Without any warning! They——" He broke off as the class bell rang.

"Perhaps I should have said outrage," Principal Bates agreed. "This morning, our students and teachers will attend an assembly in the gymnasium. We will all listen to the radio while President Roosevelt addresses Congress in Washington, D.C."

"Good," Christopher exclaimed. "He'll have plenty to say."

"I'm certain he will. This terrible attack has brought our country together as never before. In weeks ahead, we're sure to see many examples of patriotic fervor."

Macy and Christopher looked at each other. Principal Bates must have seen danger in their faces. He added in a voice that turned them both to face him, "By patriotic fervor, I mean flags and victory gardens. I do not mean fighting amongst ourselves." He looked from Christopher to Macy. "I particularly do not want to see any more fighting between students from my school. For any reason. Do you two understand?"

Macy swallowed and nodded, but she couldn't look at Christopher. Even so, she saw the tight lines ease in the principal's face and knew Christopher must have agreed, too. What else could he do, with the principal staring at him like that?

"You may return to class, Christopher," Principal Bates said. "Macy, I'd like to speak with you a little longer."

She'd been poised to dart from the room. With reluctance, she stood straighter before the principal's desk. The smug look Christopher threw at her before leaving told her that the principal's words about fighting had gone in one side of his head and out the other, whatever he might have seemed to promise.

She was sorry about his uncle and sick at the thought of dying men and sinking ships. But none of that could be blamed on the doll Mama had loved.

Principal Bates leaned forward over his desk. "Macy, I want you to remember that throughout history, wars have come and gone. After horrendous fighting and tragic deaths, however, peace always returns."

Macy nodded. None of that sounded good for Miss Tokyo, except the "peace always returns" part. And that wouldn't help if angry people destroyed the doll before peace *could* return.

A tremor ran through Macy. Papa would never agree to hide the doll. How could she make people understand that Miss Tokyo had nothing to do with the war and why her message of friendship was still important?

She stood even straighter, hoping the principal could see how much this meant to her. "Mama always wanted to go back to Japan. Every day I wheeled her chair in beside the doll, and we looked at her big book full of colored pictures of cherry blossoms and houses with paper walls. We pretended to share them with Miss Tokyo. Mama asked her . . . questions . . . and I pretended . . . to answer for . . ."

Her voice broke as the pain of losing Mama rushed through her again, not lessened at all by the months that had passed, as everyone said it would be.

"I'm very sorry her long illness took your mother." The principal's voice became gentle but firm. "For your mother's memory and for your own sake, I hope your father will put the Japanese display into storage for a time. Perhaps your brother can reason with him."

Macy nodded. Sometimes Papa listened to Nick when he wouldn't listen to her. For a moment, she let herself hope. But Papa also remembered Mama when he looked at the big doll's gentle expression and kind brown eyes.

She doubted even Nick could convince Papa to remove Mama's beloved Miss Tokyo just because people were angry with Japan. Papa would say that the people who sent the doll wanted peace and that their message was even more important now.

"You may return to your class," Principal Bates told her. "Everyone will soon be directed into the gymnasium for the president's speech."

Macy could hardly believe she was free to go. Relief rushed her into the hall and down to her classroom. Luckily, her seat was nowhere near Christopher's. She could feel his scowl all the way across the room.

Later, her class joined others in the gymnasium, whispering together while the speakers were adjusted. They grew quiet, turning to face the front of the room when they heard President Roosevelt's familiar, reassuring voice. Through crackles in the connection with the loudspeakers, he spoke of the bombing and declared December seventh to have been "a date which will live in infamy."

Infamy, Macy thought. *That means the date will always be evil in people's memory.*

Someone was standing across the room and she turned her head, wondering who would interrupt the president's message. Betsy Oshima! A teacher was leading Betsy away from her class. Was Betsy crying? What could have happened?

Macy felt all her nerves tighten as she watched the teacher lead Betsy through a back door. Whispers traveled around the gym and finally reached Macy's area.

Lily leaned close to repeat them to Macy. "Some older boys said mean things. They made Betsy cry."

"Then why didn't the teacher take *them* out?"

Lily shrugged. "She would have had to take too many."

That wasn't fair. Poor Betsy! Everyone was furious about the bombing. They wanted someone to blame. But why Betsy, who had never hurt anyone?

Another thought followed. *This has nothing to do with Mama's doll.* Macy filled her heart and mind with her mother's voice asking Miss Tokyo, "Will the cherry blossoms be in bloom this early?"

In silence, her own pretend voice answered for the doll, "Oh, no, Mama-san, not before spring." Macy stared hard at her hands, forcing tears back. Missing Mama still left a raw wound inside, but she would not cry here. She would not.

She filled her mind with memories of looking through the photographs in Mama's book. Sometimes, Papa had joined them, amused by their pretense and saying he looked forward to once again seeing Mama with cherry blossoms drifting into her hair. Then they would look at each other in a way that made Macy feel invisible but warmed inside just the same.

She knew that Papa wouldn't move the doll into storage just because people said he should. *It's up to me to save her,* Macy decided as she stood with the others to sing "God Bless America."

Students were dismissed for the day. Back in the classroom, Macy gathered her books and schoolwork. In her mind, she was already running to the museum to find a hiding place for Miss Tokyo.

The moment she stepped off the school porch, she saw Christopher Adams on the walk with a group of his friends. They all looked straight at her. Christopher's tough friend Mark smacked one fist into his open palm.

CHAPTER 4

It was too late to run back into the school. The rush of kids leaving carried Macy along. Christopher stepped forward to block her path.

Macy drew a deep breath. "What do you want?"

"The big doll." Cold fire flashed deep inside Christopher's blue eyes. "We're going to make an example of it. Why don't you go get it for us?"

Macy looked at him in disbelief. "She's not mine. She belongs to the museum. You want me to *steal* her?"

"If that's what it takes." He glanced around at his friends. They all nodded.

"I'm not a thief." She started past him, but his friends moved together, blocking her again. Macy looked around. Other people either didn't notice or didn't care. She saw Rachel Rivers poke a friend to get her attention. They both watched, smiling.

"Let me by," Macy said.

"Sure," Mark agreed. "We'll go along with you. You can go into the museum and bring that enemy doll out to us."

"No."

Christopher stepped closer. "Only a creep would protect a Jap doll today."

"I'll bet she's a spy," Mark said.

Macy glared at him, trying to hide the knot forming in her stomach. She didn't want any of them to know they were scaring her. These were boys she saw in school every day. What was wrong with them? "Get out of my way, Christopher. Mark. All of you."

Christopher stepped closer. The others crowded in on the sides. Panic swept through Macy. She lunged between two boys. They shoved her into Christopher.

"Stay off me," he said, pushing her away.

Lily's voice rose over the mutters. "Miss Lawrence! Macy needs help. Quick!"

Lily's sometime friend Rachel grabbed her arm. "Hush! Let's watch!"

But Lily's shout had scattered the boys. When the teacher reached them, only Christopher and Macy remained, glaring at each other.

"You two again!" Miss Lawrence's eyebrows rose above the frames of her glasses.

Macy exclaimed, "I was just trying to go home."

The teacher grasped their arms and again marched them into the building and along the hall to the principal's office. Stragglers leaving classrooms stepped aside and stared.

Christopher leaned around the teacher to scowl at Macy. "You're nothing but trouble. You know that?"

"Me?" She hated having people stare at her, but she couldn't let him accuse her and not answer. "You started it!"

"Silence!" Miss Lawrence snapped. "You'll have your chance to talk when you see the principal." She turned a warning look toward Macy before letting go of her long enough to open the door to the school office.

Principal Bates was no happier to see them in his office again than Miss Lawrence had been to bring them there. "Only this morning, I spoke to you two about fighting."

"I'm just trying to go home," Macy said again.

"She nearly knocked me down. For the second time!" Christopher's face flushed red as if he'd just realized he was admitting to a girl getting the best of him. "I don't fight with girls," he added quickly. "They're supposed to be ladies."

"Boys are supposed to be gentlemen," Macy told him.

Principal Bates cleared his throat and they both turned to face him. "This is an emotional time for the country. But you two promised not to fight each other. Since this is your second visit to my office today, I am forced to call your fathers."

Christopher gave Macy a *This is your fault!* look. She gave him the same look right back.

Waiting for Papa to come to the school to get her took a long, grim time. Macy twisted her fingers together while she sat beside Christopher on a bench just inside the principal's office. They took turns darting angry looks at each other, but neither dared break the silence disturbed only by Principal Bates's rustling papers and scratching pen.

Christopher's father arrived first. He was clearly

annoyed to be there and made Christopher mutter an apology to the principal and to Macy. The men looked at her as if she should apologize back. She didn't want to. She wasn't sorry. But neither was Christopher, so she crossed her fingers in her lap and said behind her teeth the way he had, "Sorry."

As he turned to the door with his father, Christopher protested, "Dad, she was wearing a Jap necklace!"

"Girls don't think the way we do, son," Mr. Adams answered. "She probably just thought the necklace was pretty."

Just pretty! Macy couldn't stay put. She jumped to her feet and called after them. "It was my mother's! It meant a lot to her!"

Mr. Adams smiled as if she had agreed with him, then said to Christopher, "You see? She wasn't supporting the Japs. It was sentiment. Girls put a lot of store in sentiment."

Macy caught her breath, but Papa came in then and she stayed silent. She rarely saw Papa's temper and wasn't eager to see it now.

Like Christopher, she was made to apologize for the outbursts on the school grounds. Principal Bates wouldn't listen to explanations. He wanted apologies and a promise of peace between the two of them, and that was all he would hear.

When she rode home beside Papa in his big touring car, Macy kept waiting for him to scold her, but he remained silent. She couldn't tell whether he was angry with her or simply thinking of museum business.

Halfway home, Papa pulled the car to a stop. Ahead, people were running into the street to join others already there.

"Papa!" Macy pressed her hands to the car's dash, feeling her heart catch. Were they gathering to stop the car the way the boys had stopped her from leaving school? Had Christopher and his father told others to make Papa destroy the doll?

"Something's going on," Papa said, opening the car door.

Macy gasped. "Papa, stay inside. Please!"

But no one was looking at their car or at them. Slowly, she realized that most people were looking away. The group had spread to both sides of the street and down the opposite way. Orange flames flashed upward from their midst. Cheering and whistles broke out. People clapped and shouted. Others raised their fists.

Papa stepped from the car. Too curious to wait behind even though excited fear darted through her, Macy followed.

"What's this about?" Papa asked Mr. Leefield from the stationery shop.

Mr. Leefield's eyes glowed as if the flames were reflected in them. "People are burning junk from Japan. There's a folding screen and a bamboo table."

Macy saw them now, a graceful leg from the table and a burning frame with a wooden egret standing beside a delicately carved water lily still visible.

Is there something wrong with me? she wondered. *Everyone's happy to see those things burn, but I want to run over and save them. What do a table and folding screen have to do with the war?*

Mr. Leefield sounded even more pleased than before. "See those porcelain shards? One couple threw in a complete set of dishes marked 'Nippon' on the bottom."

From farther down the street, Mark from school shouted, "Pop! Do we have anything to throw on the fire?"

His father's voice came clearly despite the crowd. "No, son. Why would we own Japanese trash?"

Near Macy, a man said, "Miss Markham just

added her favorite silk scarf. The thing's made from the cocoons of filthy Jap silkworms."

A woman with him said with pride in her voice, "Good for Miss Markham to throw it on the fire. She didn't hesitate even though she loved wearing that scarf. She always drew compliments with it."

She did love it, Macy knew, remembering the soft blue silk draped like a kitten around Miss Markham's shoulders. She had even let Macy wear it for a little while once. The scarf was much lighter and softer than the silk of Miss Tokyo's kimono. But she didn't dare even think of Miss Tokyo, for fear someone would hear her thoughts.

Another woman said, "She wouldn't feel right wearing that scarf again, not with our boys dying in Pearl Harbor and who knows where else."

Macy looked more closely at the faces around her, recognizing the grocer, Mr. Bradford, who often invited her to have a free cookie from the big bin with the glass lid. There was Mrs. Morris from the variety store, who loved showing her the newest items. And the men who often stood visiting outside the barbershop. All three were here now, talking in loud voices.

She knew these people. They were her friends. But today they scared her.

They'll remember Miss Tokyo, she warned herself. *They'll wonder if Papa and I are on the wrong side in this war if we don't get rid of her.* But losing Miss Tokyo would be like losing Mama all over again. Macy clutched Papa's sleeve and pressed her face into the familiar wool.

He looked surprised to find her beside him and turned her away from the crowd. "We'll take another way home. Get back in the car."

The other streets were clear. They made good time, but Macy no longer worried about punishment for fighting at school. She was too sick with worry for the doll to spare any for herself.

"Papa," she said, daring to break into his thoughts, "do you think we should hide Miss Tokyo?"

"Hide her?" Papa's dark expression made her scoot closer to the door, sorry she'd spoken. "That doll has been among the museum exhibits for years. We're not going to *hide her* because some fanatics blame everything Japanese for this war."

"No, Papa." Macy was glad. It was awful to imagine Miss Tokyo coffined away in the storeroom. It was even worse to think of angry people hurting her. "I meant maybe we should take her to the storeroom for a while."

"If we take down the Japanese display, what will people want next?" Papa demanded. "Shall we go through the museum and remove anything German? Or anything Italian? Bloodthirsty rulers in those countries are allied with the Japanese against us. Suppose other countries join the Axis. Do we purge the collection again? Tell me, how would that serve the war effort?"

"It wouldn't," Macy said quickly, giving him the answer he expected. But Christopher's threat echoed through her mind against the ashy memory of burning silk and carved wood. *We'll get rid of it. I'll get my dad to take some men over there.*

CHAPTER 5

As they passed the giant oak trees outside the museum, Macy glanced at Papa, hoping he'd forgotten he was bringing her home from the principal's office.

She jumped from the car as soon as he parked it outside the curator's house, where they lived. "I'll be right back. I just want to talk to Miss Tokyo."

She didn't wait for permission, but dashed across the green lawn to the Victorian mansion that housed the museum. She ran down the hall lined with glass cases displaying African and Native American jewelry and, gasping for breath, into the ballroom, where Miss Tokyo waited on her stand.

There was no time to admire the little china tea sets or the rosewood cabinets and silk-shaded lamps from Japan. Macy imagined she could hear the townspeople marching on the museum. She had to hide Miss Tokyo before they got there.

She grabbed a large woven basket from a Native American display, hurrying but trying to be careful as she placed all the Japanese pieces inside. She was forbidden to touch any of the displays, but she closed her mind to the rules. They didn't apply today. They couldn't. Not with Miss Markham's silk scarf blazing in her mind along with all the other Japanese items people were burning.

Miss Tokyo's dishes and lamps were the easy part. A pole behind the doll held her in place. She would have to be lifted straight up off it.

"You have to hide, Miss Tokyo," Macy murmured as she climbed onto the stand beside the doll. "Angry people are coming. They want to hurt you."

The words caught in her throat, and she swallowed hard as she tried to listen for the doll's answer. She didn't hear one, no matter how she tried to pretend. "I guess you'd rather talk about something pleasant, like the fishermen with cormorants and how the lamps on their boats light up the dark water while the cormorants dive for fish."

The memory clung, as if she still leaned against Mama's chair, looking at pictures in the big book. She imagined leaning closer over the picture of fishermen tying ropes around the birds' necks. In her memory, Mama's soft voice explained, "When the birds dive for fish attracted to the lantern light, the ropes keep them from swallowing."

"I hope they get to eat one when they're done," Macy said now, as she had then. "Because life should be fair, and if they don't get to eat a fish, it isn't fair."

It isn't fair! The words sent tears down her cheeks. They were angry tears, but she didn't know if the anger was for the cormorants, the danger to Miss Tokyo, or for the sailors dying in Pearl Harbor. Maybe the tears were all because of losing Mama.

She put her hands on each side of the doll, trying to think about Miss Tokyo . . . only Miss Tokyo. *Push her up carefully,* she warned herself. *Don't let her fall.*

From the doorway, Papa asked in a sharp voice, "What are you doing?"

Macy sank to her knees on the stand, her arms still around the doll. A sob broke through and her voice got higher than before. "People are coming to get her. We have to hide her!"

"That's plain foolishness. No one's coming here. Put everything back the way you found it. Now!"

"She's right," Nick said, stepping around Papa as Macy began setting Miss Tokyo's lamps and things beside her again. "Everyone's hopping mad. In town, they're saying anything Japanese should be dumped. Or worse. I watched Miss Markham from the bakery burn a perfectly good scarf because it was made of Japanese silk. Other stuff was burning, too. Everybody cheered."

"We were there," Macy said, "coming from school."

"You were? I was toward town with Hap."

"That doll isn't a foolish bit of silk woven to please a woman," Papa cut in. "She's a museum artifact to help educate future generations. She stays where she is."

"If they burn her," Nick pointed out, "she won't be here for future generations."

Macy sucked in a sharp breath. Nick's warning painted her memory with flames blazing upward from things people had loved. Until now.

"Letting a mob win is like paying a black-mailer," Papa said. "It never stops. As curator of this museum, I decide what is or is not displayed. The doll stays. Help your sister restore the display."

Papa spun on his heel and walked back to the entry, with its information desk.

"What can we do?" Macy asked Nick. "Papa won't listen. He never listens to me. He never even calls me by my name."

"That's because it was Mama's middle name, after her grandpa. Pop used to tease her by calling her both names, Mary Macy. And you look more like her every day." As Nick glanced around, he pushed one hand through his hair as if that might help him think.

Nick had told her before that she looked like Mama. Macy didn't think it was true. Her brown hair didn't have the golden glints that had brought sunshine into Mama's, not as many, anyway. But she did have the same green eyes and the same sort of nose, and she thought her smile was a lot like Mama's.

The front door slammed, startling her so that she nearly fell from the stand. Nick caught her and lowered her to the floor. Men's raised voices came from the entry. Angry voices. Macy looked wide-eyed at Nick. "They're here! What will we do?"

There wasn't time to do anything. The men were closer, their voices familiar. As the first man came into the room, Macy stepped forward. "Hello, Mr. Walters. How is your garden? Are your winter vegetables doing well?"

It might have sounded like a silly thing to say when the men were here to take the doll, but Mr. Walters looked startled. She thought he might be remembering the times he had cut a dahlia for her when she paused by his fence to admire his flowers.

"It'll do," he muttered. "Cabbages look good."

A second man came in, followed by a third— Mr. Bradford, who always found time to visit when Macy stopped by his grocery store. She was disappointed to see him here. Papa followed the men, arguing with them all. They ignored him. He might as well have been telling the walls about the value of museum displays for future visitors.

Mr. Collier, who worked for the newspaper, cast a searching glance around the room, ending with Macy. "Don't look so worried, young lady. We're just here to reason with your father."

Mr. Bradford added, "That big doll belongs in storage."

"I see no reason for that," Papa said, moving to stand beside Miss Tokyo.

"We've heard complaints," Mr. Bradford said. "People want the display taken down."

"The whole thing stands for the enemy," Mr. Walters said. "Our children shouldn't have to look at Jap junk."

Macy looked from one to the other, fearing what they would say next, fearing what they might do. They weren't listening to Papa. She thought they had come to the museum determined not to listen.

Mr. Collier spoke in a reasoning tone. "Putting the doll in storage for a while is part of the job of taking care of the exhibits entrusted to you. If it stays, kids are likely to go at that doll with scissors or knives."

"Or paint," Mr. Bradford said.

Papa's mouth thinned. "I have more faith in our children's respect for the museum than you gentlemen apparently do."

All three men got redder, as if he had insulted them. Maybe he had. The deepening color in their faces reminded Macy of Christopher when he realized he was complaining of being shoved by a girl.

Christopher was the one upset by Miss Tokyo. He'd complained and sent these men here. She was sure of it. She would never forgive him.

Nick shifted, and she wondered if he meant

to stand beside Papa. Would there be a fight? She knotted her hands into fists, determined to help if she could. She just wished Christopher were here, too, so he could see that she and Nick and Papa weren't going to let anyone push them around.

CHAPTER 6

From the doorway, Nick's friend Hap Davis said, "Hey, fellas, don't go picking on my doll. Miss Tokyo and I go back a long way."

He winked at Macy, and she couldn't help smiling. Hap's real name was Harold, but people had called him Happy his whole life. Nick said that was because Hap had the kind of smile that made you want to smile back. He was already eighteen, one of her favorite people and Nick's best friend.

Macy watched the anger melt from the group of men. Even Papa lost his tight look and let his shoulders relax.

Still, Mr. Collier was having trouble bringing his thoughts around. "You and a doll?" he asked, sounding incredulous.

Hap grinned at Nick. "You'd have jeered me like the rest of the first-grade class if you'd been here then. The doll was still in one of the back rooms when Miss Lewellyn took our class through. They couldn't drag me away from Miss Tokyo."

"A doll." Mr. Collier sounded even more disbelieving.

"The doll and all her little chests and lamps and stuff." Hap crossed the room to pick up a tiny silk-shaded lamp on a glowing rosewood base. "Everyone said dolls were for girls, but her things fascinated me. They still do."

He raised the lamp to eye level. "Look at this. The shade is pure silk, hand-painted with tiny lotus blossoms. This doll teaches us a lot about her country's culture."

Mr. Bradford shook his head. "All we need to know about that doll is that her country killed our boys at Pearl Harbor."

A serious look came over Hap's face. He set down the lamp and put one hand lightly on Miss Tokyo's head, as if to protect her. "My girl here had nothing to do with that. I fully doubt the artist who created her had anything to do with the bombing, either."

He looked at Macy before adding, "Any more than our Macy will have anything to do with the bombs and bullets we're about to send their way."

"That's right," Nick said. "There are a lot of patriotic fellows down at the Navy Enlistment Center. I don't believe even one of them blames this doll for the war."

Hap walked over to put a hand on Nick's shoulder. "Gentlemen, here you have the newest member of Uncle Sam's navy. And I'm proud to say that I now represent the United States Marines."

For a moment, the entire room went silent. Then Macy's shocked voice rang out. "You joined up? Both of you?"

It couldn't be true. Could it? Hap was just saying that to take their minds away from the doll. Wasn't he? The awful image of ships sinking and men in burning water flashed through her mind.

"Aren't you a little young?" Mr. Collier asked Nick.

"Pop signed the paper allowing me to enlist. Hap and I both leave for training at the end of the week."

Everyone looked at Papa. Macy saw pride in his

face and knew that Nick was telling the truth. He was a sailor now. He was leaving. He was like all the boys at school, and some of the girls. He wanted to fight in the war.

She felt proud of him and of Hap and scared to her toes for them both.

"Well, then," Mr. Walters said loudly, "congratulations, both of you. If I were your age, I'd be signing up, too, and proud to do it."

The other men quickly added congratulations of their own. "It's a fine, patriotic thing you're doing," Mr. Collier said. Mr. Bradford added, "The town can be proud of you two."

They all began talking about the military and why Nick had chosen the navy and Hap the marines and where they hoped to serve. Inside Macy, the growing coldness vanished. Instead, she felt warmth swell through her chest. She pressed her fingers to a smile on her lips. When Hap came in, everything had changed.

She moved closer to be nearer to the happiness that always seemed to be part of him. "I'm glad you came by," she told him, and added before she could hear how dumb it sounded, "When I grow up, I think I'll marry you."

He could have laughed, but he didn't. He looked

at her with the same approval he'd had for Miss Tokyo. "Great! I'll wait for you."

"I wouldn't count on that," Mr. Collier said. "You two boys will fall in love with girls overseas and likely come home with war brides."

Macy was already upset with Mr. Collier. Now she didn't like him at all.

CHAPTER 7

When Nick came in for breakfast on Saturday, the bright anticipation on his face looked like more than eagerness to head for basic training. It looked like a secret he could hardly hold back. Excitement rippled through Macy. Maybe he had decided not to catch the train this morning.

She didn't dare ask in case she was wrong, so she just said, "You look like you're expecting fancy waffles, but Miss Rasmussen's making pancakes."

"With her homemade blackberry jam? That's just what I wanted." Nick sat on his usual chair around the corner of the table from Macy. He beamed at the part-time housekeeper and cook, then back at Macy. "I have something for you, Sis. I was going to leave it with Pop for your Christmas, but I was afraid you'd notice it was missing and get upset. Besides, I wanted to be here when you opened it."

She'd been right to be excited. "What? Miss what?"

He set a small package beside her plate, wrapped in tissue paper and tied with a red ribbon. "Merry early Christmas!"

"For me?!" She looked from the package to Papa. "May I open it now?"

His smile looked almost the way it had before Mama got sick. "Go ahead."

What could be in the package? It was far too small to be a puppy or even a kitten. It could hold a goldfish, but a fish would need to be in water.

She had teased herself long enough. Feeling about ready to explode, she gently shook the package. "It's something hard. And small." She looked at Nick. "I can't guess."

"Don't guess," he said, grinning. "Open it."

She pulled the end of the ribbon so the bow untied, then slipped it off, taking her time to make the surprise last longer. Then she couldn't wait and ripped open the tissue. A familiar gold chain slipped partly into her hand. Her breath caught. With trembling fingers, she pulled the final bit of paper away. "My doll! You fixed her!"

Happy tears nearly kept her from seeing Mama's little *kokeshi* doll with her head fastened on again. Black paint covered the top where a new bun had been glued on to hold the chain.

Macy leaped from her chair to fling her arms around Nick in a fierce hug. "I thought she was ruined forever!"

"Luke helped repair her for you. Our handyman can do more than mow lawns and hang pictures, you know. He found a little dowel the right size. We got the old one out and glued the new one in the doll's head, then glued the other end inside her body, and there you are."

"Thank you! Thank you! Thank you!" Macy leaned back to look at him. "I wish you weren't going away."

He took the *kokeshi* doll from her and fastened the chain around her neck. "There. Just like new. Now give me that big smile I've been waiting to see."

She gave him her best Cheshire Cat grin, but

her smile became natural as she slipped into her chair. "You're the best brother in the whole entire world!"

Papa said, "Remember to thank Luke, too, when you see him."

"I will." She smiled down at the *kokeshi*, turning it so the doll faced her brother.

Hap's rapid code knock sounded at the back door, the way it had for as long as they'd known him. She turned toward the kitchen door as he sauntered in. "Morning, everyone!"

As the others welcomed him, Macy held out the doll. "Hap, look! Nick fixed my *kokeshi*!"

"Hey." He lifted the doll for a closer look. "I'll bet your Mama's smiling down right now, thinking she can't tell it from new."

"She is," Macy agreed. "I mean, I'm sure she is. I haven't had time to show Miss Tokyo, but I will right after breakfast."

Miss Rasmussen hurried in with a platter piled high with steaming pancakes. "Good morning, Hap."

"Morning, beautiful. Think you can find an extra plate for a hungry marine?"

"I sure can." She set down the platter and headed back into the kitchen.

Hap tousled Macy's hair before taking a seat next to Nick. "I couldn't go away," he said, teasing, "without sharing a last breakfast with my favorite girl."

For Macy, it was the best breakfast since before Mama got sick. She kept looking from Nick to Hap, almost forgetting to eat as she tried to memorize their flashing smiles and the joyful impatience in their eyes.

Hap caught her glance and grinned. "The next time you see us, Macy, we'll be wearing spiffy new uniforms. Is your imagination wild enough to picture that?"

"Yes." She smiled around a bite of pancake she had just raised to her mouth. "You'll be even more good-looking. Both of you," she added quickly, before Nick could tease.

He teased anyway. "Come on, Sis. You won't care how we look. You'll be too busy asking what we'll bring you from Japan."

The pancake dropped from her fork to her plate. "Are you going to Japan?"

"Not right away," Hap assured her. "Not until our boys chase them all the way back to Tokyo."

Nick added, "I just hope the war lasts long enough for us to take part."

Hap must have seen the worry in Macy's face. "Your brother wants it to last long enough for all the girls to see him decked out in his new uniform."

"That, too," Nick agreed.

Macy leaned back in her chair. She was so proud of them both, she could hardly stand it. She was scared for them, too. *They have to spend a long time in basic training,* she reminded herself. *The war will probably be over before they have to fight.*

They looked eager and happy. She didn't care. *The girls will just have to miss seeing Nick in his uniform. And Hap in his.*

"You're coming back," she said, breaking into a pause. "Both of you. Promise."

"We'll be back," Hap said. "Just as soon as we single-handedly win the war."

Everyone laughed and began talking again. Joke or not, Macy held Hap's promise close. She wished it were time for them to come home instead of almost time for them to leave.

A lot of people came to the train station later that morning. Macy and Papa stood with Hap's parents, while Nick and Hap's friends crowded around them, cracking jokes and remembering funny times in the past. Hap's laughter rang out, sounding as contagious as ever and making it hard to feel sad.

Near Macy, a woman said to a friend, "I believe Hap can just aim that smile of his and the war will end without another shot being fired."

Macy's worry wasn't lost on Hap. He took a moment from joking with his friends to come over to reassure her. "Don't worry, little sis. We'll whip the bad guys into shape and be home before you've had time to miss us."

"I already miss you," she said, but her words were lost in the roar of the train thundering into the station. Black smoke flew like a flag of war from its stack, while the iron wheels clanked and shrieked like imagined tank treads.

Nick came over to hug Macy good-bye. "Chin up, Sis," he said, shouting over a blast of noise and smoke from the train.

His touch felt comforting, and yet signaled his eagerness to be on his way. "Macy, everything's going to work out with school and all. Don't worry, okay?"

"I'm going to miss you."

"Write to me," he said, turning to shake hands

with Papa while friends clapped his shoulders in cheerful good-byes.

As Macy looked after him, she noticed Christopher Adams with his family farther down the platform. A young man with an expression as eager as Nick's hugged the women and shook hands with the men. He took time to shake Christopher's hand, too, pressing the other hand firmly on top.

Macy guessed the new soldier was one of several cousins Christopher had in town. When his cousin ran to board the train, Christopher buried his face against his father's shoulder. A rush of sympathy rose through her. She clenched her fingers over the repaired *kokeshi* doll necklace beneath her collar.

She didn't want to feel sympathy for Christopher Adams. Instead, she looked for her brother, who had disappeared aboard the crowded train. The sound of the whistle blowing as it carried Nick and Hap to war stayed with her all the way home.

That afternoon, Miss Rasmussen helped her sew a flag for the window. It was white with a red border and a blue star in the middle. The blue star meant that someone in the family was serving in the armed forces.

Lily stood on the sidewalk watching while they hung the flag in the front window facing the street.

"It's not straight," she called. "Move it a little to the left. Now raise it higher. Too much! Lower it a little."

"Pray we never have to cover the blue star with gold," Miss Rasmussen said, almost to herself.

"Like Christopher Adams's mother did," Lily said, moving to the first step. "When I walked past his house, she was hanging a gold-star flag in their window."

The young cousin? No, he had just left on the train. "His uncle," Macy exclaimed out loud. "The one who was at Pearl Harbor." For a moment she couldn't breathe. *That's why he was upset to see his cousin leave. His uncle won't be coming back. He must feel sick with fear for his cousin. I'm sorry I argued with him that day.*

"His uncle died from burns he got from the attack," Lily said. "He was a nice man, always cracking jokes. Kind of like Hap Davis."

Macy took a step away from her, as if that could make the words less terrible. *What happened to Christopher Adams's uncle won't happen to Nick or Hap,* she promised herself as she walked onto the porch to see the flag from there. *Our star will always be a blue one.*

Lily walked up to the porch. "A lot of families

are making these for their windows. My father read in the paper that on the day after Pearl Harbor, thousands of men across the country signed up to fight."

"I didn't know there were that many men the right age."

"Neither did the Japs," Lily said with satisfaction, then added quickly, "I mean the enemy, the Germans and Italians. . . ."

"You might as well say Miss Tokyo," Macy exclaimed. "Say Miss Tokyo didn't know so many would enlist. I didn't think you would call our doll the enemy, too."

"I didn't," Lily exclaimed. "You hear criticism in everything anyone says. I'm afraid to talk to you anymore."

Holding her head high, Lily walked down the street.

"I wouldn't hear criticism if you weren't such good friends with Rachel all of a sudden," Macy called after her, but Lily didn't look back and she didn't stop walking away.

They made up at school on Monday. "We're best friends. We're not like the . . . the enemy," Lily said, stammering a little. Macy forgave her for almost saying, "Not like the Japanese." It was war-time. She couldn't blame Lily for hating the enemy they were fighting.

"No," she agreed. "Best friends always make up."

CHAPTER 8

On Wednesday, Macy found herself waiting in line for lunch milk ahead of Christopher Adams. She tried to keep her mind on the little glass bottles in their wire rack on the school porch, where the milkman left them each day. Behind her, Christopher talked and laughed with friends. She didn't want to interrupt, but she needed to say that she understood, that she was sorry about their fight.

When she bent to unroll her nickel from the cuff of one sock, she was thinking so hard about what she should say—or not say—that she knocked the nickel loose. It rolled in a half circle and fell over beside Christopher's foot.

He picked it up and handed it back.

"Thanks." That wasn't enough. She knew it and said, fast to get it all out at once, "I'm sorry about your uncle."

He shrugged and turned back to his friends. She felt her face get hot. He didn't want sympathy. She'd known that all along. Why hadn't she kept her mouth shut? It didn't matter. She didn't like him any more than he liked her.

But later she offered him one of Miss Rasmussen's sugar cookies from her lunch box. She was glad when he took it.

To her surprise, he sat beside her to eat the frosted cookie. After a bite, he lowered the cookie to look at her. "I'm sorry I said what I did when we got sent to the principal that day."

His mother had probably told him to say that. "What about sending those men to the museum to get rid of Miss Tokyo? Are you sorry about that, too?"

His eyes widened. "I didn't have anything to do with that. What happened? Is the doll still there?"

"Yes, she's still there." Macy looked away. "And I'm not supposed to talk to you."

"I'm not supposed to talk to you, either. My dad

didn't like having to go to the principal's office to get me."

"Neither did mine." Macy felt weird sharing something with Christopher. It didn't make them friends, though. How could it?

"Someone told me you used to live at the coast," he said. "My great-uncle lives there, close to the beach. He says he breathes better with the ocean close by."

"I wish I were there now," Macy said, almost to herself.

"Why'd you leave?"

"My mother got sick. Papa said it was too wet for her at the coast, so we moved here to the valley, where it doesn't rain so much." She glanced at Christopher. "I guess your great-uncle doesn't mind the rain."

"He's a funny old duck," Christopher said, discussing their families as if they were friends. "He wears a heavy wool coat summer and winter. His tiny little house has old magazines piled everywhere. He says he likes the spiders living in the stacks."

Macy almost — not quite, but almost — giggled.

Christopher went on with a smile in his voice,

as if he'd heard the almost-giggle. "Mom wants to hire a housekeeper for my old uncle, but he won't have a stranger snooping around. Dad says he'd scare off a housekeeper the moment she set foot inside his door."

"I think I'd like him."

"You and me both. Mom thinks I'm nuts, but I get along great with the old guy."

The bell rang, ending lunch recess. Christopher stood and held out his hand. After a long hesitation, Macy got to her feet, too. She didn't take his hand, but when he opened the door into the classroom, she walked through with him.

On her way home from school, Macy stopped outside Mr. Bradford's grocery store. Until the bombing at Pearl Harbor, she had often stopped to talk with the grocer. He was one of the men who'd come to the museum to take Miss Tokyo that awful day, but maybe he hadn't really wanted to be with the others.

He'd always seemed interested in school and how her classes were going. Sometimes he even helped with a math problem that had her stumped. She missed talking with him, and pushed the door open to step inside. "Hello, Mr. Bradford."

The grocer came from behind the counter and slapped one hand down on the glass lid to the cookie bin. "Supplies are getting short," he said. "There won't be sugar for treats much longer. I can't afford to be giving away any more cookies."

His voice sounded sorry, but his eyes looked hard. His eyes said, *No cookies for Jap lovers.*

She had come to the store hoping for friendship, not cookies. The war in Stanby was far from over.

At church services on Sunday morning, everyone was polite, but Macy felt as if the love she and Papa had for Miss Tokyo set them apart.

If I can remember the good in everyone else, why can't they remember that I'm a lot more than a girl who loves a Japanese doll? I haven't changed, even if they have.

It was a relief to slide into a pew and sit next to Lily's family, as she and Papa always did. Their smiles were friendly, and Macy felt herself relax a little.

When the pastor began a sermon about loving our neighbors, Macy was tempted to glance around to see how her neighbors were taking it. Instead, she sat straight while her mind buzzed with thoughts of people at school.

"Lily," she whispered.

Lily looked over, but so did Lily's mother, with a shushing look in her eyes. Macy pulled her church bulletin close and wrote in the margin, *Why doesn't Rachel like me?*

Lily glanced at the note, then away for a long minute as if listening to the sermon. At last, she turned her bulletin and wrote along the edge: *She's jealous.*

Macy looked at her in astonishment. She wrote in the margin, *Why?*

Lily glanced at her mother, then leaned close to Macy to whisper, "Christopher. She thinks he likes you."

"Me!" People glanced her way. Macy stared straight forward and concentrated on the sermon until no one was paying attention to her. Then she whispered to Lily, "He hates me."

Lily shook her head. "That's not what Rachel thinks."

Lily's mother put a shushing finger to her lips. Macy reached for her hymnal for the final hymn, but she couldn't focus on the words. Rachel was jealous of her? Rachel, with more friends than she had time for and a mother at home? *That* Rachel was jealous of her?

Jealous over Christopher? That didn't make sense at all.

CHAPTER 9

School had let out for Christmas vacation, so on Monday, Macy and Lily walked to city hall with bags of empty tin cans. Macy explained to a lady at a desk inside, "We're collecting because the radio said just two tin cans are enough to make a syringe to give a shot of medicine to a wounded soldier."

The lady nodded. "Everyone will be asked to save tin and more if the war goes on. Tin will be needed to ship food to the soldiers overseas, too, since it's the only metal that doesn't rust."

"We'll bring more," Macy promised, but she thought of Mr. Bradford closing the cookie bin and wondered if people would be willing to give her their empty tin cans, even for the war effort.

She pulled her coat closer around her when they left city hall.

Lily glanced at the cloudy sky. "It's cold, but let's look at store windows before we go home."

By the time they'd walked a few blocks to see store windows with animated displays, light snowflakes had begun falling. The flakes added to the magic of loudspeakers playing "Jingle Bells" as they stood outside a department store window, pointing out the moving figures inside.

"Mrs. Santa's baking cookies," Macy said, watching the smiling figure with a white apron over her red dress travel on a rail back and forth from her cookie-making table to the open oven door. Santa rocked beside the fire, reading a long list of names. In the next window, elves busily loaded bright packages onto a sleigh.

"Oh, look!" Lily exclaimed, pointing. An elf in a bright-green suit and shoes with pointed toes had reached the end of his track. He turned with a painted grin as the track circled.

"He's looking right at us!" Macy said.

The mechanical elf raised one hand and waved. Lily shrieked and clutched Macy. They both giggled while the elf slowly moved away on his track to the toys waiting to be loaded onto the sleigh.

"You have a new boyfriend," Macy teased.

"Me!" Lily exclaimed. "He was waving at you!"

Laughing, they moved on to the next window. They couldn't forget the war for long, though. Posters had gone up overnight on walls and fences and even between the store's lit windows. One of them showed Uncle Sam pointing straight at the person reading it and declaring, *I want* you *for the U.S. Army.*

"Me?" Lily asked, giggling.

Macy couldn't laugh now. The next poster showed a torpedoed ship sinking into the ocean. Big words warned, *Loose Lips Might Sink Ships.*

Macy thought of Nick training to go to sea and shivered. "Almost every family in town has someone fighting. I want them all to come home."

"They will," Lily said with confidence. "Now that our boys are in it, they'll put a quick end to the war. You'll see. I'll bet they come home before school lets out for the summer."

Macy hoped so, but she'd heard Papa talking with Miss Rasmussen about the last war, the one they still called the Great War. They'd even called it the War to End All Wars. They couldn't say that anymore. Now that one was called World War I. More men had died fighting in it than Macy could even imagine. She didn't want to think about men dying again in World War II.

Nick was on a ship, not wading ashore with enemy bullets coming at him, she reminded herself. He'd be safe. He had to be! She wasn't sure what Hap would be doing as a marine, but he'd promised to be safe.

"Look!" Lily grabbed Macy's sleeve. "There's Christopher across the street with Mark. Do you think they see us?"

"They do now," Macy exclaimed. "You've dragged me almost into the street to make sure!"

As the two boys dodged a Studebaker with a Christmas tree tied to the top, Mark called out, "Christmas shopping?"

"Just looking," Macy answered, watching the Studebaker turn a corner. Papa hadn't gone out to cut a tree yet. Could he have forgotten? They'd gone with Mama every year to find a tree and shop for a special ornament, even last year, with Mama smiling from her wheelchair.

Macy understood why Papa hadn't suggested getting an ornament this year. She didn't really want one to remind her of the first Christmas without Mama, or Nick.

But everybody put up a tree. And it was almost Christmas.

Macy swung around to Lily. "Can I go with you when your father takes you to get a tree? I think Papa forgot."

Lily's eyes widened. "We've had our tree up for a week." She paused, her eyes filling with understanding. "You could spend Christmas with us."

"Thanks, but I'm going to remind Papa that we need to get a tree." Macy turned away. The boys had almost reached them. The last thing she wanted was for either of them to feel sorry for her.

As if they would!

"We're headed for the movies," Christopher said as he and Mark stepped onto the sidewalk. "There's a Groucho Marx show on."

Mark added to Lily, "You and the Jap lover wanna come along?"

Christopher elbowed Mark, but shrugged as if he agreed. Macy stuck her tongue out at both of them. A snowflake landed on it and she giggled. She couldn't stay mad with a snowflake on her tongue.

"I can't see a movie," she told them when the snowflake had dissolved. "I have something important I have to ask my father."

"About stowing the Jap doll in a closet?" Mark asked. He grunted when Christopher shoved him harder.

Lily finished checking her purse for money for a movie ticket. With a wave to Macy, she headed with the boys down the street toward a marquee glowing with neon lights.

So much for Christopher liking her. That didn't matter. Macy had to take care of something far more important than a movie.

Papa was working at his desk in the study at home when she brought in a box of ornaments from the storage room. "I'm ready to decorate, Papa. Where will we put our tree?"

He looked as if she'd slammed the door instead of elbowing her way past it with the box. "Put them away."

"Can we have just a small tree, Papa? I'll do all the decorating." She lowered the box to the floor and pulled out the first ornament. It was a little bell from Mama's childhood in Japan. It always had a special place on the tree.

Two lines deepened in Papa's forehead. "There's a war on. Things are different. We'll have to do without a lot of things for a while."

"Without a Christmas tree?" She heard her voice rise. Everybody had a Christmas tree. "Even with the war, Christmas will come."

"We don't need a tree when your brother can't be here." As Papa looked at the bell in her hand, Macy saw pain behind his eyes for more than Nick. Christmas had been a special time for all of them, but especially for Papa and Mama. Even last year, with Mama so sick, they had laughed gently together over memories brought to them by the bell.

I haven't been thinking enough about Papa, Macy scolded herself. *Every one of Mama's ornaments must make him sadder.*

On impulse, she ran to him and hugged him. "I love you, Papa. We still have each other."

She pulled away quickly when she didn't feel a response, but when she reached the door, he called, "Macy."

It sounded strange because he hadn't used her name for so long. She stopped and turned slowly, hardly daring to hope he'd changed his mind.

His eyes were shadowed, but she saw him make an attempt to smile. Maybe he was really seeing her at last. Maybe he was realizing that the two of them could make a special Christmas together.

Instead, he said, "Talk to Lily. Her folks will let

you join them Christmas Day. It will be good for you to be with friends."

"People should be with their own family at Christmas," Macy said. She understood, but felt hurt too deep to hide. How could Papa want to send her away on such an important holiday? She couldn't help adding, "Families should be together at Christmas. Under their own Christmas tree."

CHAPTER 10

Papa had turned back to his ledger. Macy didn't think he'd even heard her. With dragging steps, she went across the lawn to the museum to sit on the floor beside Miss Tokyo. "Papa says we can't have a tree. I guess everyone will have Christmas but us."

She was so used to talking for Miss Tokyo and guessing what the doll would say that words came without thought as she answered in the high voice she always gave the doll. "Nick and his friends won't have a family Christmas, either. Do you think he has a tree?"

"No." Macy stared at her fingers curled into fists in her lap. Then she raised her head. "But he can have Christmas cookies! I'll make him some. I'll make so many he can share with friends and they can all have Christmas together!"

When she ran from the museum to her kitchen, she smelled spices and brown sugar. As Macy came in, Miss Rasmussen offered a twist of paper filled with white frosting.

"There may not be a tree in this house," she said with a sparkle in her eyes, "but no family of mine is going to miss out on gingerbread men at Christmas."

Macy made a show of breathing in the spicy smells. "I love gingerbread. Nick does, too."

"Be sure to frost smiles on those cookie faces," Miss Rasmussen said. "I've seen too many turned-down mouths around here lately."

Macy knew her own mouth was curved up in a smile as happy as the ones she carefully squeezed through the frosting tube. "Let's make a lot of them, Miss Rasmussen. I want to send some to Nick to share with his friends."

"That's a wonderful idea. Your papa can't possibly object."

"He won't. It's for Nick." That was true, but Macy wished she hadn't said it out loud. A cloud seemed to pass through Miss Rasmussen's eyes. Then she put a warm hand on Macy's shoulder. "Honey, we can bake all day if you like. There's talk of rationing, but it hasn't happened yet."

"That's what Mr. Bradford said." Macy pushed down a rise of disappointment in the grocer. "Do the army and navy cooks need the sugar and shortening?"

"Not only the cooks. It's a puzzle to me, but they're saying fat is used to make ammunition."

Macy looked up in surprise. "How can fat make cookies *and* bullets?"

Miss Rasmussen chuckled. "I'm sure it's complicated, but they're telling us three pounds of fat will provide glycerin enough for one pound of gunpowder."

"What about sugar? Are they making sugar bullets?"

As Macy giggled, Miss Rasmussen rolled her eyes. "Sugar comes from hot countries like Brazil, way down in South America. I expect they need the ships to carry war goods, so they won't be able to transport as much sugar as usual."

Macy felt silly for joking. "Should we stop making cookies?"

"No, honey," Miss Rasmussen assured her. "Nothing's rationed yet. And when it is, we'll do just fine."

As Macy squeezed frosting smiles and buttons and sometimes bows or belts onto a lengthening line of gingerbread people, she hoped Miss Rasmussen was right, but she couldn't worry about the war for long. Her heart ached for a Christmas tree.

Maybe she could have one. If fat could make gunpowder, could sugar make a Christmas tree? "Miss Rasmussen," she said slowly, "last year, one of the ladies made a fancy gingerbread church for the friendship hour after service. It even had a sugar cross on the top."

"A lot of work went into that church," Miss Rasmussen said.

"I suppose it was hard and took a lot of time, but . . . do you think we could make a gingerbread Christmas tree?"

Miss Rasmussen licked a crumb from her fingertip, then smiled. "I don't see why not."

Luke, the lanky middle-aged gardener and handyman, sauntered through the outside door and leaned a narrow packing tube against a chair. "I smelled gingerbread baking all the way across the yard."

"I suppose you're planning to talk us out of a cookie," Miss Rasmussen said, pretending to sound severe.

"Or two." Luke sprawled onto the chair. "Two would be just about right with a cup of your good coffee."

She was already pouring. Macy grinned. Miss Rasmussen pretended to be annoyed by the gardener, but she liked hearing compliments to her cooking.

"Guess what we're going to do," Macy said to Luke.

"Hmm." He tilted his head as if thinking. "The two of you aren't planning to run off and join the army, are you?"

"No!" Macy laughed. "We're going to build a Christmas tree. From gingerbread."

Did that sound silly? She waited for him to tease her about baking a cookie tree, but he looked thoughtful instead. "Gingerbread? Brings to mind a tree I saw in a bakery window in Portland last year."

"Was it gingerbread?" Maybe her idea wasn't silly after all.

"No." Luke accepted a cup of steaming coffee from Miss Rasmussen and smiled his thanks for a plate holding two fat gingerbread men. "This tree was made of frosted sugar cookies. The baker set six-pointed stars together on a dowel with smaller and smaller stars all the way to the top."

"With decorations?" Macy asked, trying to imagine the tree.

"Sugar crystals sparkled over white-frosted branches," Luke said. "But I don't see why you couldn't put little birds or something on the branches, as long as you didn't eat them."

"That must have been a pretty tree," Miss Rasmussen said. She looked at Macy. "I believe we have a jar of sugar crystals."

"Can we make one? It would be so pretty!" Macy clasped her hands together. "But we don't have a dowel."

"The hardware store has dowels in all sizes," Luke assured her. "You just decide how tall you need the tree to be, and I'll nail a proper-sized dowel to a base to keep your tree standing straight and pretty."

From the doorway, Papa asked, "What tree? What's going on in here?"

CHAPTER 11

ookies, Mr. James," Miss Rasmussen said cheer-
fully. "We're baking cookies to send to Nick so
he and his friends at the training base can share
some of our Christmas."

Papa cleared his throat. "Good idea. Nick always
likes gingerbread."

Luke put down his coffee cup. "Here's your
world map, Mr. J. The stationery store was almost
out. I guess everyone's tracking the battles."

Papa opened the tube and drew out a rolled
map. "Give me a hand with this, Luke. We'll tack
it on the wall there above the buffet."

Miss Rasmussen hurried to remove a painting
of Professor Stanby to make room for the map. She

placed the painting on folded napkins in a drawer of the buffet while Papa and Luke stretched the map on the wall and secured it with tacks.

"I've been keeping a list of where troops are fighting," Papa said. "Did you get colored thumbtacks, Luke?"

The handyman brought out a small cardboard box from a jacket pocket. "Right here, Mr. J." He opened the box and set it on the buffet. "I bought map pins so the tops won't hide the names of towns, rivers, and such."

They all watched in silence as Papa consulted a list compiled from radio reports. He chose pins with red tops for enemy forces and gold ones for American troops. "It's not as current as I'd like, but censors are keeping a tight lid on news from the front."

Macy felt her heart beating faster. Just looking at the map scared her. She swallowed hard. She was glad Nick and Hap were still in training somewhere safe.

"Papa," Macy said when Luke had left, "would you help frost smiles on the gingerbread men? We're making a lot of them. For Nick."

She expected him to refuse, but he looked at the tray of cookies with a faint smile at the corners of his mouth. "It's been a long time since I've frosted a cookie."

"Then it's time you remembered how," Miss Rasmussen said while Macy held her breath. "Sit down there beside your daughter while I make up a frosting tube for you."

She picked up a triangle of parchment paper and with a few quick twists shaped it into a tube with one end open and the other a narrow point. She scooped in vanilla frosting, rolled the paper over the end, clipped the point, and handed the tube to Papa, all in what seemed like half a second.

Macy smiled to herself, thinking Miss Rasmussen hadn't given Papa time to come up with an excuse. With the frosting tube in hand, he sank into the chair next to Macy. She pushed a cookie man over to him.

His smile flickered again. "I guess I can take time to frost one for Nick."

Macy was afraid, from Miss Rasmussen's set mouth, that she was going to suggest he frost one for his daughter, too, but the housekeeper wisely stayed silent.

The next day, Macy began her tree. Luke had fastened a new wood dowel to a base. She only had to layer cookie stars over it for branches, starting with the biggest star she could fit on a cookie sheet.

White royal frosting dried like polish and sparkled with the sugar crystals she sprinkled over each branch. She was tempted to take a bite but remembered, *This will be our Christmas tree.*

The finished tree stood over a foot high, the lower branches reaching past the edges of the plate holding the dowel on its base. Macy put blobs of colored frosting on the sparkling branches for ornaments, and even found a blue sugar bird among Miss Rasmussen's decorating supplies.

"I wish I could bring it over so you could see it," she told Miss Tokyo later at the museum, "but it would be awful if I dropped it. A lot of work went into that tree." She paused before adding, "Do you think Papa will like it?"

In the doll's high voice, she answered, "Oh yes, Macy-chan. When he sees how pretty you made the tree, he will say you did a good job."

"He probably won't say it," Macy admitted in her own voice. "But maybe he'll think it."

On Christmas Eve, the tree stood proudly in the center of the table. Macy set out Mama's best china. The entire dining room seemed to glow. For

Christmas dinner the next day, Miss Rasmussen had promised to bring over some of the turkey she would roast in her parents' oven across the street. Tonight, Macy and Papa sat down to baked fish, boiled potatoes with butter, and a wedge each of iceberg lettuce topped with creamy French dressing.

Macy held her breath when Papa looked at the tree. "So you finished it."

"Yes." She waited for praise. When he looked more interested in his serving of fish, she added, "It took a lot of time."

He nodded and reached for the nearby radio to tune in the latest war news. Nick wasn't even in the war yet. Couldn't Papa leave the radio off just for Christmas Eve?

Macy didn't want to make matters worse by asking. Instead, she kept her eyes away from the war map on the wall and tried to steer the conversation to the cookie tree. "Tomorrow we can eat it. We've never had a Christmas tree we could eat before."

The radio announcer was talking about fighting in the Philippines. Macy wasn't sure Papa even heard her.

Hours later, Macy sat on her windowsill, looking out at the stars whenever the clouds broke enough to show them. She and Mama had always claimed the brightest one as their own Christmas star. Nick teased that they were claiming a planet, but it didn't matter. It was bright. It was beautiful. It would do.

There! That was the one. She blew a kiss toward the sky and whispered, "Do you see our star, Mama? Of course you do. Let's make a special Christmas wish together, the way we've done ever since I was little. This year, I'm going to wish for an end to the fighting so Nick and Hap can come home."

She watched the star, wishing with all her heart. When she realized tears were rolling down her face and that she was cold in her nightgown, she reached for the window to pull it shut.

Then, she added to Mama, "I've been talking with Miss Tokyo, telling her all about the Christmases we used to have and the one we're having now. It's different and sad without you and Nick here, but we're doing all right, Mama: Papa and me and Miss Tokyo. Don't worry about us."

Even so, when she woke on Christmas morning, instead of jumping to her feet as she usually would, Macy pulled the blanket over her head. What was the point of getting up when Mama and Nick were gone? There wouldn't even be a real tree with Mama's ornaments on the green branches and presents underneath.

Through the blanket, she smelled Miss Rasmussen's pancakes. On special days, the house-keeper grated chocolate into the batter. Macy smelled chocolate now. She couldn't help smiling as she pushed back the blankets.

Sure enough. She could see the dining table through the doorway as she came down the stairs. A plate heaped with pancakes waited beside the cookie tree. Macy drew in a deep breath of warm chocolate and crispy-edged pancakes. "That smells so good!"

"I was about to call you," Miss Rasmussen said from the kitchen doorway, "but I knew the pan-cakes would do that for me."

Macy drifted into the dining room, following the sweet aroma. She stopped in surprise. The pancakes were not alone beside the cookie tree. A book-size package wrapped in gold paper also waited there.

CHAPTER 12

Macy slowly moved closer, almost expecting the package to vanish before her eyes, but she wasn't imagining it. A tag with Mama's handwriting read, *For my dearest Macy.*

Her eyes misted suddenly. She couldn't even reach for the package, still fearing that it might vanish at a touch. "Is it . . . for me? Really?"

Papa answered as he came into the dining room. "When your mother knew she would not be here to share Christmas with us, she asked me to save this for you." He hesitated, then added, "She would have enjoyed your little cookie tree. It seemed right to put her gift beside it."

Macy reached out with shaking hands and slowly untied the ribbon. She felt as if Mama had heard her message in the stars and reminded Papa of the gift. For a moment, she held it close, feeling close to Mama.

When she removed the bright paper, she found a leather-bound journal with her name on the cover in gold. Inside, a note in Mama's flowery writing said, *My darling, I hope you will remember the fun we've had together and share those memories with our Miss Tokyo whenever you open this little book.*

Blinking through misty eyes, Macy said softly, "Mama used to say that even when times are hard, we can always find something to be happy about. I'm going to do that. I'm going to write in my journal every day. I'll write notes to Mama and read them to Miss Tokyo, so Mama can hear them."

"There are a couple of cards for you to open after breakfast," Papa said. His eyes looked bright, as if he held back tears, but his smile remained steady. "Your mother wanted you to have her gift first thing this morning."

Mama never could wait, Macy remembered, swallowing a lump in her throat as she returned Papa's smile. Mama had always wanted to open gifts the moment they came downstairs. Papa insisted on breakfast first, but sometimes gave in to opening just one gift before even tasting Miss Rasmussen's special pancakes.

Now Macy felt as if Mama were here, sharing Christmas with them. She stroked the cover of the new journal, happy that Mama's gift was the one opened before breakfast.

When at last the dishes were washed and put away, Papa offered two red envelopes, each with Macy's name on the front, the first in her brother's familiar scrawl. She wrote often to Nick. He wrote back when he had time. These two cards were like special Christmas presents. She opened the first, giggling at a cartoon of Mickey and Minnie Mouse waving U.S. flags from inside a Christmas wreath.

A flash of silver fell from the card. She scooped it from the table. "Look, Papa, a little silver anchor on a chain."

She opened the card to find a note. *The boys won't want to rip this one from your neck. Wear it proudly for your brother in the U.S. Navy.*

"I will!" she said, as if Nick could hear her.

While Miss Rasmussen helped her link the chain behind her neck, Papa pointed out the second red envelope. "There's another. Looks like it's from Nick's buddy."

"Hap?" She breathed his name, hardly daring to believe he'd sent a card, but there was his name up in the corner.

"It's like Hap to remember this would be a sad Christmas for you," Papa said.

She hardly heard him as she pulled the flap loose. Hap had mailed it from the marine boot camp in San Diego, California. She wondered how long it had been here without her suspecting.

This one made her laugh, too. "Look, Papa. Santa's in a flying navy ship, dropping presents down chimneys."

She couldn't tell Papa that Hap was going to be her husband someday. He'd call her silly and remind her of the age difference, but it didn't matter. Hap had promised to wait for her to grow up.

She sat beside Miss Tokyo's stand to write the first notes to Mama, reading aloud as her pen moved. *Dear Mama, thank you so much for the pretty journal with my name on the cover. I love it, just as you knew I would. It made Christmas special even though we are all missing you.*

Nick sent me a little silver anchor on a chain. I'm going to wear it every day, so everyone will know I'm as patriotic as they are.

She looked up at the doll. "Do you think she heard me?"

"Oh yes, Macy-chan," the doll answered in her pretend voice. "Mama is pleased to hear that you love her gift. She misses you, too."

The doll's voice broke in a sob. Macy didn't say any more, for fear her voice would not be steady, either. Christmas without Nick and Mama was too hard to think about. It should have been a day to spend with family, so when Papa decided to dust and polish everything in the museum, she worked beside him. When she straightened Miss Tokyo's kimono and smoothed the doll's black hair, she felt Mama nearby.

It was good to keep busy, but when vacation was over, she was glad to return to school. Most of the girls admired the silver anchor and even some of the boys said it looked swell. Macy was happy to report to Mama that the anger so many had turned on her after Pearl Harbor had begun to fade.

She stroked her fingertips over her name embossed in gold on the cover of her new journal. The soft leather felt welcoming, as if warmed by her mother's touch.

CHAPTER 13

In school, the teachers explained that the town would be holding blackouts for the duration of the war. If the warning siren blew, everybody had to turn out their lights within sixty seconds.

"Most of your parents are installing blackout curtains," Miss Stewart told Macy's class.

"Will those let us keep lights on inside the house?" Lily asked.

Miss Stewart nodded. "Blackout curtains won't allow light to pass." She walked around her desk and leaned against it. "Each of you must help. It will be your part of the war effort to check every window for your parents to make sure the curtains are tight and that no light comes through along the sides or bottom."

"Why?" asked a girl in the back who had been whispering to a friend instead of paying attention.

One of the boys turned to scowl at her. "To keep enemy planes from seeing light and knowing where to drop their bombs, dummy."

"Are enemy planes coming here?" The girl jumped to her feet as if ready to run but not sure which way to go.

"Sit down, Amy," Miss Stewart said. "We have people watching the skies. No enemy planes have been seen. We mean to be ready just in case."

Mark laughed. "Yeah. We don't want to be like Amy, running around calling, 'What? Where? What am I supposed to do?'"

Miss Stewart made the class stop laughing and take the blackout seriously. "It's going to be very, very dark outside, especially when clouds block out the moon."

Christopher grinned. "Sounds like a good time to go around to girls' windows and make scary noises."

Mark laughed. "I can already hear them screaming!"

Again, Miss Stewart called for order. Macy

glanced over at Lily, who had become silent and very pale. "Don't worry, Lily. Those boys won't have the nerve to go out in the dark to try and scare us."

She wasn't sure that was true, but Lily looked relieved, and Macy was determined to be brave.

Another girl raised her hand. "My dad read in the paper that we might have to paint the White House black so enemy planes won't see it."

Mark grinned. "They'll have to change its name, too. We'll have to start calling the White House the Black House."

Macy asked, "Is that true, Miss Stewart? Are they thinking of painting the White House?"

"I've heard that rumor," the teacher answered, "but the people in Washington, D.C., don't agree." She glanced around the room. "How many of you believe the White House should be painted?"

Several raised their hands. When Miss Stewart asked how many believed it should be kept white, more hands went up. "Leland," she said, "you voted for black paint. Why do you believe that's a good idea?"

"So enemy planes can't see it."

She nodded and asked, "Macy, why did you vote to keep it white?"

"There are a lot of white buildings in Washington — the Capitol and others. They represent our country. We should be proud of them and not hide them from anybody."

"*You* should hide," a girl said from behind her in a low voice. It sounded like Rachel. "Nobody likes you anymore."

Macy refused to turn around to see if it was Rachel being mean, but the back of her neck felt tight, as if her skin were braced against possible spitballs. She kept her hands on her desk even though she wanted to clasp the *kokeshi* doll she still wore beneath her collar to feel closer to Mama.

In a louder voice than usual, Lily said, "After the war is over, black paint would be really hard to clean off the white marble."

"That's a good point," Miss Stewart said, and called the class to order again when everybody started talking. "One more thing. The school will be holding a scrap drive. I expect all of you to urge your mothers to save empty tin cans and extra cooking fat."

Amy raised her hand. "What about the old cannon in the square? It's not good for anything and it's made of solid metal. Can we donate that?"

"No!" the boys exclaimed, while several girls looked horrified.

Christopher said, "That's part of history. It's from the old fort outside of town way back from when we were still a territory instead of a state."

Miss Stewart raised her hand to stop a dozen protests. "There are no plans to melt down any of our memorials."

Leland said, "I'll bet we'll have to if our country gets invaded!"

"For now, we'll leave the old cannon where it is," Miss Stewart said. "Please collect whatever scrap metal you can find."

In her letters to Mama, Macy began counting the days until Nick would come home on leave after training to be a sailor. *Only ten more days, Mama.*

Now we only have nine days to wait until Nick comes home.

It's seven days . . . five . . . three . . . !

Nick came home on leave on a blustery day in early February. Rain slanted into the rail station on gusts of wind while Macy waited with Papa for Nick's train. When one of the gusts carried the lonesome sound of the train whistle, she raced outside onto the platform.

Iron wheels screamed down the rails. The engine slowed and cars clattered past, moving more and more slowly. Macy scarcely felt the rain or the wind as she jumped up and down, trying to see into each window. Men were crowded into every seat and standing in the aisles. It was impossible to see her brother.

The wheels finally ground to a stop. People crowded from inside the station onto the platform, eager to greet returning servicemen.

For a moment, Macy didn't recognize the sailor stepping from the train in a white uniform and cap, with a duffel bag slung over one shoulder. Then he saw her and grinned. She ran shouting to meet him. "Nick! Nick!"

He dropped the bag and swept her high. "Hey, Sis!"

He whirled her around and set her down, marveling. "You weigh almost as much as my seabag. And you've grown taller! Have I been away so long?"

She hugged him with all the fierce love churning through her. "Yes! I miss you more now than on the day you left!"

Laughing, he tousled her hair. "You wouldn't want me to hang back and not do my part." He glanced around. "Where's Pop?"

"Back there." She stepped away, wiping her eyes. Nick waved before swinging the bag—his seabag, she reminded herself—onto his shoulder again. Together, they wove through the people still crowding the platform.

Papa came to meet them, his hand outstretched. "Welcome home, son. It's good to have you back."

Macy couldn't remember ever seeing Papa's whole face light up with a smile like the one he had as he and Nick clasped hands.

Hap came home the next day. When he came by to visit, Macy watched him talk with Nick and Papa and saw that Hap and Nick were both changed. Their eyes held a faraway look, as if part of them were already off somewhere fighting the war.

That look made her shiver. Mama would have said a goose had crossed her grave. But later, when the sun came out, she walked to the drugstore soda fountain between her brother and Hap. They wore their uniforms, and she felt proud and excited to walk with them. She hoped everyone she knew would see them together, especially the people who hated Miss Tokyo.

Nick asked her about that. She tried to make it sound funny even when her smile wouldn't stay in place. Both Nick and Hap pressed her shoulders and said she was the one in the right. Miss Tokyo had nothing to do with the war.

They had such a short time at home, and the days flew by. Hap spent most of his time with his family, and Nick was often over there. Far too soon, they were both at the rail station again, waiting for the train. They couldn't say where they were going, but everyone knew they would soon be fighting in the war.

Macy fought back tears and tried to smile. To her surprise, Hap pressed an envelope into her hand. "Happy Valentine's Day," he said, and was caught by friends crowding around to say good-bye.

She waited until she was alone at home to open the card and laughed out loud at a picture of a fuzzy dog wearing a helmet and holding up a rifle with a flag hanging from the end. The flag said, *A Valentine Hello!*

Inside, Hap's writing was kind of scrawly, and she frowned to make it out. *Happy Valentine's Day to a brave girl. I'm counting on you to win the fight at home and take good care of Miss Tokyo for me.*

Macy pressed the valentine to her cheek when she saw that Hap had drawn a heart and signed his name inside.

"I promise," she told him softly. "Miss Tokyo

will be waiting for you when you come home again, Hap. I'll be waiting for you, too."

It was hard to think about schoolwork with both Nick and Hap gone again, this time not to train but to fight in the war. When she sat at the table after dinner with her books spread in front of her, Macy couldn't stop studying Papa's map of the world and its colored map pins.

All those pins showed where men were fighting in Europe and getting shot or bombed. A shiver ran through her. Blue-star flags were in many windows now. Papa said it would just be a matter of time before they saw more gold-star flags like the one for Christopher's uncle Ray, who had died at Pearl Harbor.

Macy jerked to her feet and grabbed a blue-painted pin from the box. "This is Nick's ship," she told Miss Rasmussen. She studied the big map on the wall. "I'm going to put it where Nick will be safe."

Would that be in the middle of an ocean? Maybe enemies were watching the coastlines. Miss Stewart had talked about shipping lanes. Those would be well known, though. The enemy would know them. They might not be safe for Nick.

Papa spoke from the doorway. "What are you doing?"

Macy stabbed Nick's pin into the ocean near Australia. "This is Nick's ship. I'm putting it where he'll be safe."

"You know that won't help Nick. And it makes a joke of my map. His ship is certainly not off the coast of Australia. Take out the pin."

Macy didn't budge. "Then where is his ship?"

"That information is classified." Frown lines deepened in Papa's forehead. "You've seen the posters saying that loose lips sink ships. If people knew where our ships are sailing, word would eventually get back to the enemy."

Macy stood in silence for a moment, studying the map with Papa. "They'll come home, won't they? Nick and Hap? When the war is over, they'll come home."

"No one knows ahead of time how any battle will go." Papa gazed at the red and gold map pins he had placed in Europe. "A famous Civil War general once said that war is . . . terrible."

Macy was pretty sure the general had used stronger language, but it meant the same thing. She looked at Papa, waiting for the answer he hadn't given her. She needed to hear that Nick was coming home.

When Papa remained silent, Macy's entire body seemed to tighten, as if pulling away from anything hurtful. Papa wasn't sure Nick and Hap would ever come home. He was like Lily in some ways. He had pretended Mama would get well, but he couldn't pretend now. He wouldn't say what wasn't true.

Macy used her sleeve to wipe tears from her cheeks.

She felt Papa's hand, warm and strong on her shoulder. "I can promise you this much. If at all possible, when this war ends, they'll be on the first ship home."

Macy was able to breathe again. Papa still thought that day might come.

He pulled out the blue-headed pin. "Even if we knew where Nick's ship was, we would not mark a spot on the map. Your friends might tell somebody and they'd tell somebody, and eventually Nick's location could reach the enemy." Papa dropped the pin into a wooden box on the buffet. "The map is not a toy, Macy. Remember that."

He gathered some papers from the table and left the room. Macy stared at the map with its tiny hole where her pin had been.

Gently, Miss Rasmussen said, "He worries about Nick. We all do."

"That's why I'm keeping Nick safe." Macy located the blue pin, glanced after Papa, then chose a spot off the coast of California and settled Nick's ship firmly in place. "There. He's almost home."

She sat at the table and opened her history book. Having Nick safe, even if it was a kind of pretend, made homework go faster.

CHAPTER 14

Early in the spring, Betsy Oshima and all her family were told to pack what they could into one suitcase each. They were told to board a train and travel to an internment camp in Arizona. Papa explained that anyone with even one-sixteenth Japanese blood would have to spend the length of the war in a special camp.

"They'll be safer there," Papa told Macy. "Remember how . . . angry . . . people have been about Miss Tokyo. There will be even stronger feelings against the Oshimas. They'll be at risk if they stay on their farm here."

"That's not right," Macy protested. "After Pearl Harbor, when we were all in the school yard pretending to shoot Japanese planes, Betsy was right there with us, pretending, too. She's not from Japan. She was born right here. So were her parents."

"It's war. A lot of things aren't right."

Macy couldn't accept Papa's answer. On the day the Oshimas and other Japanese families were to leave, she walked to the station, wishing she had talked more with the girl, even though Betsy was a year younger. She stood beside a pillar, trying to see Betsy. She wanted to tell her she would miss her.

Families crowded the platform, wearing their best clothes and carrying suitcases packed with all they were allowed to take with them. Macy brushed tears from her cheek. They were leaving farms where many had lived their entire lives. Who would care for their crops? Who would feed their chickens? And their dogs? Betsy Oshima had a dog. Where was it?

Japanese people with worried or set expressions filed into waiting railcars. As the train rolled slowly ahead, Macy moved closer to see who was near the windows of one car after another. By the time a fifth car had rolled past, she realized that smudges on the train's sides were from fresh dirt clods. Someone must have been throwing them farther down the track.

She didn't have time to see who was doing that. The fifth car carried Betsy in a seat beside a window, looking out with a sad expression.

Macy ran even closer, waving her hand so Betsy would see her.

The girl leaned near the window. A smile brightened her entire face. She waved just as hard as Macy, pressing against the window to keep in sight longer as the train kept rolling.

When Macy wrote to Mama that evening, she told her about the Japanese families sent away on the train, adding, *I'm glad I went down to wave good-bye. Nobody else did, except somebody throwing dirt clods. Betsy seemed glad to see me. I still don't understand why she had to go.*

In early April, Macy located the blue-headed pin in the box where Papa had tossed it again and walked over to the map. Where would be a safe place for Nick today? Maybe he'd like Canada. She pushed the pin high in the north between Canada and Russia.

Papa came in as she opened her notebook to begin an essay for her English class. He studied the map, asking, "Where is Nick sailing today? Ah, off the coast of Canada. I'm afraid his admiral has a poor understanding of maps." He dropped the blue pin back into the box, but he chuckled.

Macy smiled to herself. When Nick left for the war, he had said that she and Papa would become closer with him gone. It was true, but Nick couldn't have known it would happen over a blue-headed map pin.

Miss Rasmussen brought Papa coffee to carry over to his desk at the museum, then glanced at Macy's empty essay page. "What does your teacher want you to write about?"

"My favorite pet." Macy leaned her cheek on her hand and stared at the paper. "I don't have a pet. Maybe I can write about Miss Tokyo."

The housekeeper dried her hands on her ruffle-edged apron and considered. "You must have friends who have a cat or dog or even a goldfish. Why don't you write your essay on what you like about one of those and maybe how you'd treat a pet like that and what you'd call it. There's lots you can write."

Macy chewed her pencil, thinking.

Luke sauntered in through the back door with a load of firewood. He dropped it into the wood box and grinned at Miss Rasmussen. "Thirsty work."

Miss Rasmussen took a clean cup from the dish drainer and poured coffee into it. "Sit down, Luke. Maybe you can give Macy a hand. She needs to write a school essay about a pet."

Luke sank into a chair near Macy and sipped the hot coffee. "The Oshimas' dog. Now there's a story. They couldn't take it on the train, you know. Had to leave it behind on the farm."

"Who's feeding it?" Macy asked.

"As it happens, I drove out there a day or so later just to see where that dog might be."

"Was it there?" She held her breath. She had wondered about Betsy's dog when the Oshimas had to board the train without it. "Why didn't you bring it here?"

"I thought about it." Luke sipped his coffee again, drawing out the story. "The Johnsons' oldest boy was hoeing weeds when I drove in. You know the Johnsons, from the next farm south. He said his family's keeping care of the Oshimas' crops for them."

Miss Rasmussen said, "I'm glad to hear that. I hope all the interned Japanese have good neighbors caring for their crops."

"But what about the dog?" Macy asked.

"The dog was with the boy, bouncing around

chasing butterflies. He's staying over at the Johnsons' until his family comes back from the camp."

"That's a good story." Macy bent over her paper and began to write. She made a mistake and started to reach for an eraser before she remembered she didn't have one anymore. "Luke, did you know we get all our rubber from the Dutch East Indies?"

"Well," he said in his teasing voice, "I didn't think it grew with our strawberries and grapes."

"It grows on rubber trees," Macy said. "But the Japanese captured the Dutch East Indies. So now we can't get any more rubber for erasers and stuff." She looked up, her eyes widening. "Erasers are against the law!"

"The rubber shortage is why Mr. Bradford isn't delivering groceries anymore," Miss Rasmussen said. "He can't get new tires for his truck."

Macy looked at the word she had misspelled and carefully drew a line through it.

"Your teacher won't think kindly on a messy paper," Luke warned.

"She has to. Miss Stewart says not giving erasers to students saves thousands of pounds of rubber for the war effort." Macy studied her paper. "Miss Stewart said she won't mark us down if we cross mistakes out carefully."

"We're living in strange times," Luke said. "I heard ladies can't buy nylon or silk stockings anymore. The soldiers need nylon for parachutes and silk for powder bags, since it won't cause sparks."

"You're well informed," Miss Rasmussen said.

Luke grinned. "Ladies are even drawing lines down the backs of their bare legs to look like stocking seams."

His grin widened when Miss Rasmussen put on a disapproving expression. Macy wasn't surprised when he kept teasing. "No more twisted seams for you ladies. That'll be a boon, won't it? Tell you what, Miss R., anytime you want to borrow my calipers to hold a pencil steady, just let me know."

"The nerve!" Miss Rasmussen exclaimed. "Talking about ladies' legs in front of the girl!"

Luke chuckled as he finished his coffee and left. Macy covered her smile with her hand so Miss Rasmussen wouldn't think she was laughing at her.

CHAPTER 15

When sugar rationing began in May, Macy walked with Miss Rasmussen to the school gymnasium to stand in line with many other people. "It's part of the war effort," a woman in front of them said. "This is the least we can do for our brave soldiers."

Macy agreed. She would stand in line all day and all night if it would help Nick and Hap. "I won't use sugar on my oatmeal anymore," she told Miss Rasmussen. "Then we can save enough coupons to buy sugar to make fudge for Nick."

"That's a generous idea," the housekeeper said

with a smile. "But we can't save stamps. We have to use them every month and throw away any we have extra."

From across the gym, a woman called, "Sally Ann Rasmussen!" A blond woman hurried toward them. "I haven't seen you since high school!"

They hugged, then Miss Rasmussen stepped back, smiling. "It's been three years since I graduated. You were two years behind me and you look prettier than you did then, Patty."

The other woman's eyes sparkled. "That's because I'm excited! I'm going to Seattle! I'll help build airplanes in the Boeing plant and make heaps of money."

"Seattle! You were going to study to be a teacher. What does your father say?"

"Oh, you know fathers. They get grumpy when they don't get what they want." Patty winked at Macy. "I'll bet you're one of his students. I should be careful what I say!"

"My teacher is Miss Stewart," Macy said, confused.

Miss Rasmussen explained. "Patty . . . Patricia . . . is Principal Bates's daughter, honey." She turned back to her friend. "Isn't this idea kind of sudden?"

"Who has time for long debate? Say, why don't you come with me? We can be roommates. Put away money for our old age. Maybe meet the men of our dreams."

Miss Rasmussen shook her head. "The men of our dreams are all fighting in the war."

"But they go on leave. We can help out at the USO when we're off work. We'll serve the boys coffee and doughnuts and maybe share a dance. Come with me, Sally Ann. It will be swell!"

Macy saw temptation in Miss Rasmussen's face. Was she really thinking of leaving them to go work in the Boeing plant and dance with soldiers and sailors? She tugged the housekeeper's hand. "Papa and I need you here."

Miss Rasmussen seemed to shake the dreaminess from her expression. The ration sign-up line was moving forward. "That's not for me," she told her friend. Clasping Macy's hand, she stepped forward with the line.

"Think about it," Patty said before leaving to join friends across the room.

"I'll do that much," Miss Rasmussen called after her, making Macy feel cold inside. "I might not be able to think of anything else!"

In early June, Macy sat beside Miss Tokyo, writing a note to Mama in her Christmas journal. *Miss*

Rasmussen didn't go to Seattle with Principal Bates's daughter, but she left us anyway.

You'd be surprised, Mama. All around the country, women are signing up with the WAAC. That's the Women's Army Auxiliary Corps. Last week, Miss Rasmussen joined! When she left, she said she'll miss us, but she wants to serve our country even if they only allow WAACs to do paperwork. Papa says maybe she'll meet somebody nice and come back married. Luke doesn't like that idea, but we're all proud of her for helping the war effort. We'll really miss her, though.

Macy closed the journal and hurried to the kitchen to help Papa with dinner. It didn't take long. Their meals were simpler now without Miss Rasmussen. Neighbors sometimes brought extra servings from their own meals, and that helped.

When they'd finished, Macy carried their dishes to the sink, then turned to study the big map on the wall. Papa was listening to the radio and moving map pins around.

He hadn't yet noticed the blue pin for Nick's ship, safe in a cove off New Zealand. Macy ran water into the sink for the dishes, smiling as she waited for Papa to notice the blue pin.

The news switched to a commentator whose

voice rose a little as he reported, "A military man says that death and destruction may come down from American skies at any moment."

When Macy gasped, Papa turned the radio down. "Don't believe all these reporters, Macy. Some of them think they need to scare people so we'll support the war effort."

She shivered. "We're already supporting the war as much as we can! They have Nick and Hap. And now they have Miss Rasmussen!"

The radio commentator's words made fear almost crush her. She had learned to push it back most of the time, but not always. Leaving the dishes to soak, she rushed across to the museum and Miss Tokyo. She knelt beside the doll's stand and looked into her gentle face. "Is Mama listening, Miss Tokyo?"

"Yes, Macy-chan," the doll said in her high voice. "Mama always listens to you."

"Please tell her I'm so scared for Nick. So is Papa." She drew in a deep, shaky breath and spoke straight to her mother. "We're trying to be brave without you, Mama, even though it hurts."

Macy bit her lip and waited a moment until she trusted her voice again. "We just can't lose Nick, too. So if the angels tell you Nick will be with you soon, please tell them we need him here. Ask them to please give him more time. Let him come home to us after the war."

Papa sat at the breakfast table one morning when school had let out for the summer and turned on the radio. "We're not getting a lot of museum visitors these days. With gas rationing and the risk of wearing out their tires, people are staying home more."

Macy poured the coffee she had made just the way Miss Rasmussen did and carefully carried the cup to him. "Will the museum have to close?"

He sipped the coffee and nodded approval. "Not right away, but fewer visitors will give us time to do a better job of polishing floors and dusting exhibits. There will be a small salary for you if you're willing to help."

"Of course I'll help." She would help without a salary just to work with Papa, but it would be nice to have spending money.

Busy days passed quickly, she found. It was mid-July before she had time to sit beside Miss Tokyo and write a quick letter to Mama. *It's been fun working with Papa. Everyone in town seems nicer this summer. Maybe they aren't mad at Miss Tokyo anymore. Maybe they aren't mad at me.* She hoped that feeling would last, especially when school began again in the fall.

After Labor Day in September, she used a lot of exclamation marks in her note to Mama. *School started again! I'm in sixth grade! We're still at war, though. So it's still scary! The littlest kids have to hide under their desks when the siren blows. They hope the desks will protect them if bombs fall!*

Older students are supposed to run to nearby homes when the siren blows. I hope I get assigned to a family that likes to play Monopoly so we won't have to think about bombs!

We haven't heard from Nick for a while. Maybe I should stop moving the pin for his ship around. I don't think he gets near land long enough for the crew to send the mail!

She didn't tell Mama that the hope for friendlier feelings hadn't lasted. Mark and Rachel had begun saying mean things about Miss Tokyo again. Macy didn't write those things to Mama. She didn't want to say them in front of the doll.

She did tell Mama about the Evil Axis. *That's what they call our enemies, Japan, Germany, and Italy. Christopher Adams got so mad at news about Adolf Hitler that he threw his mother's German nutcracker men in the trash. His mother made him dig them out and scrub them, but she stored the nut-crackers away until after the war.*

When Christopher told the class about it, he stared straight at me. As if he expected me to stand up and say we were putting the Japanese doll in storage. I guess he's been listening to Mark and Rachel. I don't care what any of them think. Miss Tokyo is my friend.

Macy sat with Lily on their favorite bench outside the schoolroom with their lunch bags on a windy day. Macy smoothed a letter from Nick on her knees, trying to keep the wind from catching it. "The paper he uses is so thin, I can almost see through it."

"Airmail paper," Lily agreed.

"And look," Macy said. "One side of the paper is the letter, then he folds all the sides in and writes the address on the back so it turns into its own envelope. That way it doesn't weigh much and the mailbags can carry lots more letters to families."

"If you don't know where he is, how can you write back to him?" Lily asked.

"He uses an FPO address. That means Fleet Post Office. The people there know where to send it."

She looked up as Christopher walked over. "A letter from your brother?" he asked.

"Yes." Macy spread Nick's letter on her lap, careful to keep it safe from the wind. "He can't say anything about where he is, but he loves the feel of the waves."

She stopped. "The censors used a black pen to cover whatever he said next." She grinned. "I'll bet he said he almost never gets seasick. When we lived at the coast and he went fishing on trawlers, he always bragged about that. Why would the censors care?"

"They're very careful," Lily said. "My father was upset when they canceled his favorite radio program, the one with interviews with 'the man in the street.' But he said he'll agree with anything that keeps our boys safe, and an interviewed man in the street could easily be a spy using the radio program to send coded information to our enemies."

"They're even censoring weather reports," Christopher agreed. "The radio can't mention rain or snow or fog or even sunshine because it might help the enemy." He watched Macy smoothing Nick's letter on her lap. "You've had a letter from your brother every day this week. You're lucky."

"He thinks about us a lot."

Lily sighed loudly. "It's the same letter. She brings it every day and pretends she just got it."

Lily was her best friend, but *honesty* might as well have been her middle name. Macy could only bite back tears and say, "You don't know everything."

"I know that's the same letter," Lily said.

Christopher broke in. "I'll bet he does write every day, but the mail doesn't get off the ship that often. You'll probably get a bunch of letters all at once."

From across the school yard, Rachel called, "Christopher! Do you want to hear something funny Mark just said?"

Macy looked after Christopher as he walked away. Could it be true? Would a bundle of letters be coming from Nick? That had to be what was happening, and she was going to answer every letter, one at a time. She turned to ask Lily if she thought the letters should be numbered in case Nick got them in the wrong order.

Lily was watching Christopher join his friends. "Rachel's right. He does like you."

"What? Who? Christopher! No, he doesn't." But he had given her hope about Nick, and today she couldn't even resent Rachel.

In October, dried leaves crunched beneath Macy's shoes when she walked home from school to share good news with her mother. She went straight into the museum and over to Miss Tokyo and pulled the Christmas journal from under the doll's stand, where she kept it.

Guess what, Mama, she wrote. *We collected lots of scrap iron and tin over the summer. The school set up a collection in September and Principal Bates announced a contest. The class that collects the most scrap before Christmas break will win a trip to the skating rink in Junction City!*

Rachel's already teasing the boys about skating with her. She promised to teach Lily to dance on skates. I don't care. I just want to go skating. I hope our class wins!

Macy couldn't understand why Lily wanted to be with popular, flirty Rachel. She told herself she didn't care.

Every day for two weeks when Macy walked home from school, she slid her shoes along the pavement, pretending to be wearing roller skates and practicing moves. Thinking that Nick and Hap would laugh at that, she glanced at Hap's house as she passed. His mother stood in the big front window, placing a gold-star flag against the glass.

The air whooshed out of Macy's chest. She

clutched the pickets in the fence. That didn't mean . . . It couldn't mean . . . No!

She should ask. . . . She didn't want to ask. . . . Asking might make it true. And it couldn't be true.

She was scarcely aware of Mark crossing the street until he stood close to her and asked, "What do you think of your Jap friends now?"

"What?" she asked, too numb to think.

"Your friends," he repeated, sounding even meaner than usual. "Your Jap friends. You know. The ones fighting our boys on Guadalcanal. They killed Hap."

She stared at him. In her head, she understood what he'd just said. In her heart, his words didn't make sense. "No," she said. "No!"

"Yes! One of their sneaky crew threw a grenade. Hap dived on it to protect his friends. It ripped out his guts."

Macy dropped to her knees, leaning into the nearby weeds to throw up until nothing was left inside her. Grief swelled through her chest. There was no room left for air. Gasping and clutching the pickets for support, she struggled to her feet. To her own ears, her whimpers sounded like a small wounded animal.

"I guess that makes Hap a hero," Mark said

in the same nasty voice. "I say it makes him stu-pid. I'll bet his friends all ducked out of the way."

Macy had room for another emotion after all. Hot anger blazed through her. Without thinking, she reached for one of the decorative rocks under the pickets.

"What are you gonna do with that?" Mark asked. "You gonna hit me?"

Macy straightened up. "I'm going to knock your lying teeth out of your mouth."

As she swung her arm back, the house door opened, revealing one of Hap's neighbors. "Children," the woman called. "Play somewhere else, please. We need quiet."

The interruption gave Macy time to think. Mark wasn't worth the trouble she'd been about to bring on herself. She let the rock fall.

"Get rid of that doll," Mark said, and walked away.

Macy looked at the woman on the porch. Should she ask if what Mark had said was true? No. The gold flag and request for quiet told her all she needed to know.

Tears welled through her. Turning, she ran for home. *She had to talk to Miss Tokyo and Mama.*

She veered into the museum, shoving past the

heavy front doors. Her father stood quickly from behind his desk.

Macy cried, "They killed Hap."

She ran down the hall to the doll and fell sobbing to her knees. *"Mama,"* she said between sobs, *"I can't grow up and marry Hap. The war killed him."*

She raised her head to look at the doll. The gentle eyes looked sad. Instead of an almost-smile, her lips looked as if she were about to speak. But she was silent.

"Hap loved you," Macy told Miss Tokyo. "He knew the war wasn't your fault." Her voice broke, and she lowered her head to her arms on the doll's stand. Beneath grief, deep fear hovered, no matter how she tried to push it down. If Hap had been killed, what was happening to Nick?

Despite her love for Miss Tokyo, she hated the generals who had caused the war that killed Hap and was killing a lot of other men. Who might kill Nick. No! She would not even think that. Despair boiled through her. Mama's book held beautiful pictures of shrines and flowers and pretty ladies in kimonos.

But men from Japan had bombed Pearl Harbor. They were killing men on islands in the South

Pacific and on ships in the waters around them. Grief for Hap wrenched her. Again, she pushed back the fear that Nick could be killed, too. Her thoughts spun until they made her dizzy.

Her father's strong arms lifted her into his lap. He held her, not talking but stroking her back and hair, comforting her in silence while anguish tore away her thoughts.

Finally, she curled close with her head on his shoulder. "I'm so scared," she whispered.

"I know," he said. "We all are."

Standing, he carried her from the museum and back to their kitchen. While she slumped on a chair, wiping tears from her face with a kitchen towel, he made hot chocolate for both of them and added a few hard-to-find marshmallows.

Without speaking, they watched their marshmallows melt into the chocolate. When Macy stood to locate Nick's blue-topped map pin and place it in the safety of San Francisco Bay, Papa didn't protest.

CHAPTER 16

Three men came in when Papa opened the museum on Saturday morning. Their message was clear before a word was spoken. Neighbors, Macy thought, and yet today they were strangers. She stepped backward, closer to Papa.

The men's eyes were cold. Their mouths were set in dangerous lines. She had never seen them like this. She wanted to run but was afraid to move.

Mr. Broward stepped forward. Before the war, he had been a cheerful man behind the butcher's block who picked out special cuts for Miss Rasmussen. He was clearly in charge of the group, but there was no doubt that all the men were set on a single purpose.

Mr. Ames from the gas station put it into words. "We're here for that Jap doll, James. Step aside."

Mr. Bradford had been with the first group, months ago. The grocer had changed from the kind man she had known all her life. This was what war did, made strangers out of friends, even when battles weren't being fought in your town.

"That doll stands for people who are killing our boys," he said. "Hap Davis defended the doll. And look what happened. The Japs killed him. Word's all over town."

The pain of Hap's death struck Macy as if new to her. The gold star in his family's window seared her memory. She'd been too shocked by her own grief to realize that anger was building in others.

"Everyone in town is torn up over losing Hap," Mr. Broward said, breaking into Macy's thoughts. "We want to see somebody pay, here and now. The Jap doll will do. A bunch of folks are building a bonfire in front of the courthouse."

Did they mean to *burn* Miss Tokyo? Macy looked to Papa for help. His eyes were hard and angry, but he said nothing. She thought he must have said it all the last time men came, but then they'd only wanted to put Miss Tokyo in storage.

"Her kind isn't wanted here," Mr. Ames said. "She'll burn. For Hap."

Papa wrapped one arm around Macy, pulling her to his side. She realized she had taken a step forward without thinking. Papa's hold told her it was too late. He said to the men, "Burning the doll won't help Hap."

"We've formed a committee," Mr. Bradford said. "We're set on keeping our city safe."

"The doll is no danger to this city," Papa said. "Neither is the museum."

Macy looked from one to another of the men. None looked willing to listen to reason. She knotted her hands into fists so tight, her nails dented her palms.

"That Jap doll puts us all at risk," Mr. Broward said, his eyes looking even harder.

"She probably has a secret radio inside," Mr. Ames snapped. "She's probably radioing the Jap fleet right now." He glanced around as if expecting enemy soldiers to smash through the Stanby's doors.

Papa said, "I think you know how foolish that sounds. If you're looking for a reason to destroy city property, you'll have to do better."

Mr. Bradford asked, "Is the museum's safety

reason enough for you? The longer that Jap doll stays here, the more riled up people get."

Mr. Ames cut in. "Hap Davis getting killed is all it took. There's talk of burning the whole blasted Stanby to the ground."

Macy felt Papa stiffen. She clutched his sleeve. "Papa!"

"Go to the house," he said without looking at her. "See to supper. I'll take care of this."

"There's nothing to take care of," Mr. Broward said, "except for you stepping out of our way."

Macy looked toward the room with Miss Tokyo, frantic to get to her. Papa gripped her shoulder, turning her toward the back door.

Despairing, she looked up at him. "Papa."

"Go home, Macy," he said. "Now."

He'd used her name, but it made her feel worse, not better. He was going to let them take the doll and didn't want her to see it. She knew he couldn't fight them all and maybe even the whole town. But Miss Tokyo was her friend! In Macy's heart, Miss Tokyo held part of Mama! Papa felt that way, too!

"Go," Papa said again, sounding as hard as the men.

There was no choice. She rushed down a hall

past the stairs to the storage room and out the back door. A light rain was falling. She scarcely felt it. A storm raged inside her head.

When she reached the steps to the house, voices made her turn and look back. The three men were leaving. Mr. Broward had Miss Tokyo over his shoulder as he might carry a slab of beef. The long ends of the doll's obi whipped in the wind.

Macy clamped one hand over her mouth to keep from screaming. Her heart slammed so hard in her chest, her ribs hurt. She had to run after them, to stop them somehow.

What could she do? Grabbing the banister, she forced herself one step at a time up the stairs, away from the men taking Miss Tokyo to be burned.

As if a rubber band had released her, she rushed into the house and up to her room. Anguished tears streamed down her cheeks. She flung herself face-down on the bed.

"I loved Hap, too," she said with a sob. "I was going to grow up and marry him. And now I can't. Because he's dead. But that doesn't make me want to burn down the museum!"

She reached across the bed to her nightstand and the valentine from Hap. For a moment, she pressed it close, as she had done countless times before. She pictured Hap's carefree grin and the kindness in his eyes.

"I loved him," she whispered. "I really, really did. I don't care if I am only eleven."

She could almost hear Papa calling her foolish. Everyone would think that. It was why she had never shared the valentine with Papa or anyone else.

She opened the card and read the words she had memorized long ago. Then she looked at them again, really looked at them. Possibilities raced through her head so fast they made her dizzy.

The men would make speeches before they burned Miss Tokyo. Mr. Ames loved to make speeches. And he'd want a good crowd gathered while the bonfire blazed higher. Maybe they hadn't even lit it yet. Maybe people were still bringing wood while Mr. Ames excited them with his speech.

Urgency drove her to her feet. "They'll listen to you, Hap. They'll have to!"

Clutching the valentine in one hand, she scrambled from the bed and raced for the stairs.

CHAPTER 17

As she ran down the street, Macy heard Mr. Ames shouting. He was making one of his speeches, all right. Papa called him inflammatory. He sounded now as if his words could light a bonfire all by themselves.

As she came closer to the courthouse, she saw the bonfire that people were building in the street, mostly of sticks and firewood, but with at least two kitchen chairs thrown in. She had hoped the rain would put out their fire. Instead, it had stopped, letting sunlight touch the heap of wood.

Mr. Ames's voice became clearer: "We all know the Japs will come. We've heard it on the news.

They're coming, all right. They're coming here with bombs and guns!"

Macy caught herself glancing at the sky and mentally pinched her arm. She had to keep her mind on what she knew was true. Miss Tokyo needed her. Where was the doll?

She glanced past the bonfire and saw Miss Tokyo lying in the grass beside the sidewalk, her legs sticking out of her kimono. She didn't look graceful now. She looked abandoned. For a moment, Macy wondered if she could sneak over, grab the doll, and run. She pushed the thought aside. Even if she got away with Miss Tokyo, she would just be putting the problem off for a little while.

"We all know the Jap farmers came here and planted their farms to point to airports," Mr. Ames shouted. "We know the Japs on the coast arranged their fishing boats around our harbors, watching which ships came in. Before we shipped them off to internment camps, they reported those ships to their bosses."

Macy had heard those rumors on the radio. Papa said they were foolish and just excuses for sending people like Betsy's family away to camps ringed with barbed wire.

"What about that big doll?" someone shouted.

A woman answered. Macy recognized Mr. Ames's wife. She echoed his warning from the museum. "She probably has a secret radio inside. She's probably broadcasting to Japan right now."

"Cut the Jap doll open!" a man yelled.

"Let's see what's inside," another called.

Feeling desperate, Macy looked from one to another. Hap's parents stood in the first row with friends around them. Their eyes were red, but they held themselves straight, with their shoulders squared and their heads high. Hap would have been as proud of them as they were of him.

"Where's an ax?" someone yelled.

"NO!" Macy's loud shout startled even herself, but she got attention. Several people turned to look.

She walked right up to Mr. Ames. "Why are you doing this? For Hap?"

"You bet it's for Hap," Mr. Ames said loudly. "That brave boy gave his life to keep us safe from the Japs. And from Mussolini's thugs and from Adolf Hitler's goose-steppers."

"That doesn't have anything to do with Miss Tokyo!" Macy yelled back.

"Go on home, little girl," someone called from

the crowd. "That doll's going to burn for what the Japs did to our boy."

"Hap didn't want her to burn," Macy shouted back. "He didn't want anything bad to happen to her."

"Shut your mouth, girl," Mrs. Morris called from across the bonfire. "Nobody wants to listen to a kid."

"Will you listen to Hap?" Macy held up the valentine she had never shared with anyone. The valentine was private, but she didn't care if they thought she was silly to love Hap when she was only eleven. What they thought of her didn't matter anymore. "Hap gave this to me for Valentine's Day when he was home on leave. This is what he wrote inside."

Hap's writing was kind of scrawled, but she knew the words by heart. She read them in her loudest voice, to reach even the people at the back of the crowd. *"Happy Valentine's Day to a brave girl."*

She paused to look around the crowd, making sure they were listening to Hap's words, then brought her attention back to the card. "He wrote, *'I'm counting on you to win the fight at home and take good care of Miss Tokyo for me.'*"

She held up the card. "See! He drew a valentine heart and signed his name inside."

Mrs. Davis looked as if she were fighting tears. Macy felt sorry to make Hap's mother even sadder, but maybe they were memory tears and she'd feel better for letting them out.

Mr. Broward came toward her. "Let's take a look at that."

It was hard to let the card out of her hand. The Christmas card and the valentine were all she had of Hap. What if they put it into the fire?

"She won't show it," a woman shouted. "She wrote it herself!"

Mr. Davis left his wife to come toward Macy. "We know our son's writing. Let me have a look."

She wanted to tell him how sorry she was about Hap, but it didn't feel like the right time. In silence, she handed the card to Hap's father.

He read to himself, his lips moving as if he murmured the words so low no one could hear him. Then he walked back to his wife and offered the card to her. Tears spilled from her eyes and ran down her cheeks, but she reached out a trembling hand.

She took the card, glanced at it, and pressed

it against her chest. "It's Hap. My boy wrote this. He . . . he wanted to save the doll."

Others asked to see the card. Mr. Davis took it gently from his wife and handed it around a circle of doubtful people.

"I promised I'd look after her," Macy said. "I promised Hap."

No one was paying attention to her. They were all looking at the valentine or talking with Hap's parents.

Then Hap's mother said in a voice that trembled but stayed firm enough to be heard, "Hap was fascinated by the doll's accessories. I'd forgotten! He was only six the first time he saw them. He came home and talked for days about all the little furniture and the silk lamp shades made by real silkworms way off in Japan. I . . . I guess he never forgot about that big doll."

Hap's father spoke in a no-argument voice. "We won't be burning that doll. We won't go against one of our boy's last wishes."

Mrs. Davis left the people around her and came to Macy, holding out both hands. Gently, she took Macy's hands in hers. Tears made her eyes shiny and her cheeks wet, but she smiled. "Thank you. You've

returned a memory I'd forgotten—we both had—
when every memory we have of him is precious."

Macy saw that people were leaving, walking
toward their homes. Some of them looked as if
they'd been sleepwalking and were surprised to find
themselves out in the street.

Macy lifted Miss Tokyo, hoisting her high on
one hip. "I'm taking her home now."

"Go on, then," Mr. Ames said in a gruff voice
that might have been disappointed. "But keep her
out of sight, you hear?"

Miss Tokyo was heavier than Macy remembered. Six long blocks home stretched out forever.
As she walked, the doll slipped on her hip. She
hoisted her again and then again.

Finally, she sat on the curb to rest. "I don't care
how much you weigh," she told the doll, her voice
fierce. "I'll keep you safe. I don't care if my arms
fall off."

Stumbling to her feet, she tried to lift Miss Tokyo
to her hip again. From behind her, Christopher
Adams said, "Want me to carry her for you?"

Should she trust him? What if he meant to
throw the doll into the street? She took a step
toward home. Again, the doll slipped on her hip.

Christopher caught Miss Tokyo before she could hit the sidewalk. Deciding to risk trusting him, Macy let him lift the doll from her. She would simply walk close enough to snatch her back if he tried anything.

CHAPTER 18

As they walked along the street, Macy realized that Christopher was risking teasing or worse from his friends. He kept glancing around, but he didn't hand back the doll until they reached the museum stairs.

"Are you looking for Mark or Rachel?" Macy asked him as she took the doll. "Were they supposed to show up and pull some mean trick?"

Christopher looked startled. "There's no trick."

"There usually is," she said, feeling awkward. She had insulted him. He'd only meant to help. That was hard to believe. "Why are you helping? I thought you hated me."

"I don't hate you." He started to turn away, then swung back. "Remember when the Japanese were sent away on the train?"

"Of course I remember! I went down to the station to wave good-bye to Betsy."

"I know. I saw you."

"You did? I didn't see you."

"I went with my dad." Christopher kicked one shoe against the bottom step. "He wanted to make sure the Japanese left. I . . . was throwing dirt at the train. I ran after it all the way to the station."

"I was at the station."

"I know." He stared at his shoes for a moment, then raised his head. "Betsy was looking through the train window, crying. Then her face turned bright and happy with a smile. When I looked at the station to see why, I saw you there waving, showing her she still had a friend."

"She did." Macy remembered the dirt clods smeared on the train cars. For a moment, anger rushed through her. Christopher threw those! At Betsy!

"I dropped the dirt clod I was holding," he said, not looking at her. "I felt like a creep. You showed me what friendship is. And you reminded me that Uncle Ray bought strawberries from the Oshimas' farm. He didn't hate them. And they weren't the ones who bombed Pearl Harbor."

Macy's anger vanished. She didn't know what to say. She should thank him for carrying Miss Tokyo home.

But before she could find the words, his cheeks flushed red. "You should put the doll out of sight," he said, and ran off as if he couldn't get away fast enough.

"Boys," Macy said softly to Miss Tokyo. "Sometimes they don't make much sense."

"Most of the time," Miss Tokyo agreed in her high pretend-voice.

Macy hugged her. Christopher had been kind. And the doll was safe from the bonfire. That was what mattered. Papa would be proud to learn she had saved the doll for the museum.

As she came through the Stanby's big doors with the doll, Papa looked up from his desk, then sprang to his feet. "I thought you were in the house! Did you follow those men? How did you get the doll?"

"I saved her," Macy said. She expected praise, but Papa came around the desk looking angry instead of proud.

"You might have been hurt. Those men . . .

People are too angry to think straight. Don't you realize that? You heard them! They'll be coming after her again and they'll be even madder!"

"You don't understand. Hap gave me a valentine when he was home on leave. He wrote inside that I should take care of Miss Tokyo."

"He was just being friendly. He sure didn't mean for you to go chasing after angry people bent on burning her!"

"They were going to burn her *because* of Hap, Papa! I let them read his note in the valentine. When they saw he didn't want them to hurt her, they let me bring her home."

Some of the fear left Papa's face, but he glanced at the doors as if expecting a crowd to burst through, demanding Miss Tokyo. "They're not thinking straight," he said again. "They'll come after her. They've wanted to burn her for a long time. Hap was an excuse. If they can't use his death, they'll find another reason."

"No, Papa. Hap's mother thanked me, and his father said they wouldn't hurt the doll because Hap didn't want them to."

Papa's mouth was pressed tight and white around the edges. Macy knew he was thinking about what she'd said, but he was still worried for her and for the doll and maybe for the Stanby. Maybe he was remembering the threat to burn down the museum.

"This finishes it," he said. "The doll is going into storage. Right now."

Macy held the doll closer. "No, Papa. Hiding Miss Tokyo is like agreeing with those men. They're saying all the Japanese are evil. Doesn't that mean Mama's love for the people she knew was a lie?"

A startled look crossed her father's face. "There's a lot of your mother in you." He lifted Miss Tokyo from Macy and studied her critically. "After today's treatment, it's a wonder she still looks as nice as she does."

His face set with decision. "We'll display her in the ballroom where your mother wanted her. The burn-the-doll gang scattered the accessories. Come along and straighten them."

As he carried the doll toward her stand, Macy followed, her heart filling with pleasure. Papa thought she was like Mama. And he had loved Mama more than anything. Maybe something good had come from today's scary bonfire after all.

In the ballroom, she located the scattered tea sets and other accessories the men had knocked aside. When she picked up a tiny lamp with a silk shade, she paused. In her mind, she imagined Hap as a six-year-old boy, fascinated by a shade of silk made by worms in faraway Japan. "You saved her, Hap," she whispered, and carefully set the lamp where it could be seen.

When Papa left, Macy located her Christmas journal and wrote a note to Mama. *Men came to the museum and took Miss Tokyo. They said they were a committee to keep our city safe. They were going to burn our doll on a bonfire.*

Hap and I saved her.

CHAPTER 19

On Monday morning, Miss Stewart announced to the class that she might have a surprise for them by the end of the day. She wouldn't say any more, so guessing flashed in whispers and notes throughout the classroom. The most popular idea was Rachel's, who guessed that their class was to be declared winner of the scrap drive skating-trip contest.

During the lunch recess, Mark got into a fist-fight for telling a seventh-grade boy that his class had won the skating trip. They were both sent to the principal's office.

"I think she should just have told us," Lily said, watching the two boys being marched toward Principal Bates. "All this secrecy is causing trouble."

"She shouldn't have said anything at all," Amy said. "Then she could have surprised us with good news."

Lily added, "Or not tell us at all, if the news is disappointing."

When they returned to class after the last recess, Miss Stewart welcomed them with a smile. Lily whispered to Macy, "The news must be good."

When everyone was seated and looking expectantly at the teacher, Miss Stewart said, "I've had excellent news in answer to the surprise I mentioned this morning."

Again whispers circled the room. Mark exclaimed, "I told that big kid we won!"

Miss Stewart rang her bell for silence. "Now," she said. "I know you must all have been as alarmed as I was by yesterday's bonfire in the city square. The people of Stanby are better than that."

Leland said, puzzled, "Better than what? They just wanted to burn that doll."

"Precisely." Miss Stewart gazed around the room, her expression severe. "They wished to destroy an artifact that has long been a treasured gift to our museum. I asked myself why."

She rang her bell for silence when several children started to speak. "I answered my own question.

Violence often stems from ignorance. Therefore, I have arranged with Mr. James for our class to spend fifth period today on a visit to the Stanby Museum."

Macy heard people muttering that this was supposed to be about the contest, not a stupid museum. The back of her neck tensed. She could feel angry stares, but she was as surprised as any of them. She wanted to leap to her feet and say visiting the museum was a bad idea.

Miss Stewart thought it was a good idea. "Mr. James will escort us through the displays of our town's treasures and explain why each is important to our understanding of this locale and, in many cases, of the larger world."

"What about that Jap doll?" Mark asked.

Miss Stewart frowned. "The doll called Miss Tokyo was a special gift from the children of Japan long before the fighting between our countries. She tells us of the gentler and more beautiful side of her country's heritage."

Rachel said, "She's a symbol of our enemy!"

"We have not always been enemies," Miss Stewart reminded her. "This war, like all others, will end. Someday we may well be friends again. In the meantime, today we will explore the Stanby

Museum with Mr. James. I'm sure I do not need to remind you to treat all the displays with respect."

When the entire class marched down the sidewalk toward the museum, Macy ran ahead. She burst into the museum, shouting, "Papa! Papa!"

"What is it?" Her father jolted to his feet behind the reception desk. "What's happened?"

"The sixth grade," she said, gasping for air. "They're coming here. Right now!"

Papa's big chair creaked on its rollers as he eased back into it. "Oh, yes. Miss Stewart wants her students to understand how the museum enriches the community."

"We need to hide Miss Tokyo!"

"From sixth-graders? Why?"

It was too late. Miss Stewart and the remaining twenty students were coming up the stairs. Macy rushed into the ballroom to Miss Tokyo. "Don't be scared," she told the big doll. "Miss Stewart won't let anybody hurt you." She hoped that was true.

Her entire body stiffened as she heard Miss Stewart shush loud voices. "You are not small children. I don't have to remind you to enjoy the displays with your eyes, not your hands. Everyone, please stay together."

Papa welcomed the class the way he always did, teasing a little about the mummy in the Egyptian room. "This was Professor Stanby's private home before he built the nearby second home now used for the curator's family. He decided his collection needed its own space when Mrs. Stanby began using the sarcophagus for a coffee table. The mummy's still upset about that, so to assure our visitors' safety, we keep his lid tightly shut."

While Miss Stewart paused in the hallway to talk with Papa, the group came into the ballroom. Most of the class was laughing, but some wondered aloud if Papa was joking or telling the truth about the mummy. Three of the girls shrieked when Mark and two other boys said they were going to slide the mummy's lid open and see if he moved.

"What if he sits up?" Lily asked.

Rachel added, "What if he wants to know who's been putting their feet on his lid?"

Two more girls shrieked.

"We'll slam the lid down," Mark's friend Leland answered.

Mark added, "Right on his head."

Miss Stewart called the group together and warned them again about treating the exhibits with respect. "These are our town's treasures."

"That's no treasure," Leland said, pointing to Miss Tokyo. "That's the enemy that's killing our boys."

Macy had meant to be quiet but couldn't. "She is a treasure. She's here for friendship. She shows us how kids our age live in her country. Kids like us aren't making war."

"How do you know?" Rachel demanded. "They might be in workshops building bombs right now."

"Yeah," Mark said, moving closer to Miss Tokyo. "This thing might be hiding a bomb. Let's pull her ugly coat open and see."

"It's a silk kimono," Macy protested. "There's nothing inside. She's carved from a solid piece of wood."

"Come on, Mark," Christopher called. "Take a look at these arrowheads."

Miss Stewart stepped through the doorway. "Did everyone see that long chain of white seashells in the hall? Those are wampum. They were used as money."

Papa added from beside her, "We're told the museum's chain of wampum is long enough to buy a horse."

While Papa returned to the wampum display with Miss Stewart and several students, Mark snatched one of Miss Tokyo's delicate porcelain teacups and raised it to his mouth. "Oh, no! I'm drinking Jap poison!"

"Put that down!" Macy exclaimed. "It's not here to play with."

"Arghh!" Mark fell to his knees, clutching his throat, then glared up at Macy. "No, it's not for play!" He slammed the cup onto the stand beside Miss Tokyo's foot.

Pieces of fine china flew. Macy felt her insides shatter along with the teacup Mama had used in their pretend teas with Miss Tokyo. It was nothing now but shards and porcelain dust.

Christopher grabbed Mark's arm. "What are you doing, dummy? This is a museum."

Macy hardly heard him. She scooped up pieces of the cup and held them close to her cheek. Her heart ached. She thought she caught a faint scent of green tea, but that was impossible. She and Mama had never put tea in the little cups.

Mark stabbed a finger toward her. "Look at the Jap lover, crying over a broken Jap cup!"

Choking through anger and a cloud of feelings that made thinking impossible, Macy hurled the china fragments at Mark.

"Ow! Look, I'm bleeding!" Mark shouted. "That Jap lover cut me with her Jap cup pieces."

He wasn't bleeding, but Macy felt she was, inside. As she sank to her knees, Miss Stewart hurried in, demanding an explanation. Lily told her what had happened. Macy could hardly hear her through a sick roaring in her ears.

Somehow, Papa was there, lifting her to her feet. "I'm going to ask your class to leave."

"I am so sorry!" Miss Stewart clutched Mark's arm with a grip that looked painful. "This boy is going straight to the principal's office. If I might just use your telephone?"

While Papa directed her into the hall, several of the other students complained about wanting to see the mummy. Macy scarcely heard any of it. She leaned both hands flat on Miss Tokyo's stand and listened desperately. But Miss Tokyo wasn't saying anything.

Macy straightened to watch as Miss Stewart's heels tapped smartly across the polished floor. The teacher marched Mark to Papa's desk in the front hall, where she dialed the phone with quick angry jabs, then tapped her foot as she waited. When the secretary answered, she asked to speak at once with Principal Bates.

"Mark Wayfield has disgraced the entire

school," she told the principal. "He will be in your office to explain in less than ten minutes."

She slapped the receiver in place and aimed Mark toward the doors. "Go! If you are not there within ten minutes, Principal Bates will expect your father to explain why."

"My father doesn't like Japs, either." Mark spotted Macy watching through the open ballroom door and stuck out his tongue before swaggering from the museum.

Papa removed a broken teacup handle from under Miss Tokyo's stand where Macy had missed it. She could see from the sorrow in his eyes that he was remembering Mama. *War hurts everybody in all kinds of ways*, she told herself. *Why do we have to have it?*

After sighing deeply, Papa told the remaining students that he had decided to let them continue their tour. His words sounded automatic as he said again that Professor Stanby had wanted girls and boys to enjoy his remarkable collection, gathered from all over the world.

Few of the students were listening. Rachel came closer to Macy. "First it was Christopher. Now Mark. Are you going to get all the cute boys in trouble?"

Macy looked at her in disbelief. "I didn't do anything."

Rachel's mouth twisted. "I didn't do anything, either. For instance . . ." She walked around Miss Tokyo to the back. "I didn't do this! Oh!"

Macy didn't have to look at Rachel to know she had tried to pull loose the doll's obi. "It's sewed together," she said. "Mama did that to keep *kindergartners* from untying it."

"Really? Maybe I just need to pull harder."

"Knock it off, Rachel," Christopher said.

"Why?" she snapped. "Do you think Macy's *pretty?*"

"I think making Macy feel bad won't end the war any faster." He walked after the rest into the Egyptian room.

"Everyone hates her," Rachel called after him. With one hand, she brushed back her hair, then added, "If you're going to take her side, don't ever ask me to kiss you again."

Again? Macy felt as if she had fallen into Alice's rabbit hole. Everything was changing and nothing made sense.

In the next room, stone grated over stone. Macy looked at Lily, who was standing nearby. They both recognized the sound. Boys had slid aside the lid to the sarcophagus.

Papa's voice rose in anger. Papa never raised his voice to visitors. Of course, their usual visitors didn't peek inside the sarcophagus.

Across the room from Macy, a vase shattered. One of the girls said, "That looked Japanese to me."

Lily shouted, "Allison, why did you do that?"

Allison said again, "It looked Japanese."

"This does, too." Another girl hurled a carved wooden elephant. In horror, Macy watched a tusk fly free.

"I'll get your father," Lily shouted, and raced toward the Egyptian room.

Like wildfire spreading, one classmate after another chose something to destroy, calling it Japanese. Leland grabbed a velvet drape hanging beside a window and swung on it, howling like Tarzan.

"Stop!" Macy shouted.

Papa rushed in from the Egyptian room while Miss Stewart ran from the reception area. The teacher echoed Macy's scream. "Stop! Stop right now! All of you!"

Macy darted to Miss Tokyo and wrapped her

arms around the big doll. "She came here to make friends! Why can't you see that?"

"She's a Jap," Rachel said.

"Enough of that," Miss Stewart snapped. "Everyone line up. Right now!" She brought the students into order with the no-nonsense manner of a drill sergeant Hap had described on his one leave at home.

Macy was allowed to stay to help her father straighten the museum. She watched from a window as Miss Stewart marched the rest of the class at a fast pace back to school.

"I wonder how they'll act in class tomorrow," she said to Miss Tokyo.

"Don't worry, Macy-chan," the doll answered. "They know they brought trouble on themselves."

They should know, Macy told herself. But she had noticed that kids in trouble usually looked for someone else to blame.

CHAPTER 20

Macy dreaded facing Papa at dinner after the disastrous class visit to the museum. To her surprise, her father smiled as he took his seat. Miss Rasmussen's mother had carried over a big pot of beef stew half an hour before and left it to warm on the back of the stove. Macy filled bowls for each of them and carried them to the table.

"I thought you'd still be mad." The words were so close to the tip of her tongue that they slipped off before she could stop them.

Papa breathed in the aroma of the stew while Macy paused beside the map to choose a new safe place for Nick's ship. "Mad?" Papa asked. "No. In fact, today's behavior served a purpose."

The radio on the table spoke with the solemn voice of Papa's favorite announcer, Edward R. Murrow, but Papa didn't seem to be listening to the news about Americans and Japanese still fighting for the island called Guadalcanal.

Macy stabbed the blue pin into the map, tried not to think of Nick or Hap, and took her seat across from Papa. "A purpose? What do you mean?"

"The Stanby's record keeping has been lax for years," he said, ignoring the pin she had placed between Florida and Cuba. "This afternoon, I tried to assess the damage done. The Stanby's list of artifacts donated, lost, or damaged is all but unreadable."

Macy chewed a bite of beef from her stew, waiting for Papa to explain.

"I found notes in the margins," he said, "and others crowded between lines. Many entries were written in an early style that is more decorative than readable. In addition to notes jotted in, I found many cross outs. It's a real mishmash."

"Maybe if you read the notes and I write them on a fresh sheet of paper," Macy suggested, "we can put them in order."

"We'll do better than that. It's past time for a thorough inventory. I'm going to close the Stanby's doors until that's done."

Papa gazed at her for a long moment, his eyes solemn, then sighed. "Our vandals today convinced me that it's time to store Miss Tokyo and her accessories. Even with the Stanby's doors locked, I no longer feel the Japanese exhibit is safe in the ballroom. As long as our countries are at war, we'll put the doll in the storeroom. I want you to help me after dinner."

Macy felt cold inside, but she knew that Papa was doing the right thing. Even Nick would agree if he were here.

In the morning, Macy reached her classroom as the first bell rang and slipped into her seat. Miss Stewart stood at the blackboard, writing an assignment with quick screechy movements of her chalk. Her shoulders looked stiff.

She's still angry. Macy braced. Even if a scolding wasn't meant for her, she didn't want to hear one.

They were halfway through geography when the classroom door opened. Principal Bates stepped into the room.

Oh, oh. Macy sat straighter and curled her hands together on her desk. She wasn't to blame for the destruction in the museum, yet when the principal came in frowning, she felt guilty. Everyone was silent, even the ones in the back who usually whispered and passed notes.

Principal Bates paced across the front of the room and back to the teacher's desk. "You all know why I'm here."

"Because we wouldn't all fit in his office," Rachel whispered.

The principal stared at her. "What was that, Rachel?"

"Nothing, sir," she said quickly.

Macy waited for the principal to insist that Rachel repeat her comment. Instead he looked at the entire class. "I am disappointed in all of you. Yesterday's behavior is not acceptable in a sixth-grade class from this school."

No one said anything. After a pause, the principal asked, "Why was it not acceptable?" He pointed to Amy. "Do you know?"

Macy thought it sounded as if Amy were talking to her desk instead of the principal when she answered in a low voice, "Things got broken."

Principal Bates tapped one finger with another. "What else?"

Leland said, "They were treasures."

"Town treasures entrusted to our museum were

damaged or destroyed." Principal Bates pressed his lips together as if not trusting words he wanted to say. "What else?"

Rachel said in a tone that was not at all sorry, "We made Macy cry."

Macy caught her breath. Rachel had made her sound like a crybaby.

"What else?" the principal asked.

Macy raised her hand. "Miss Stewart was embarrassed."

The principal tapped another fingertip. "Your teacher wanted to give this class an interesting and educational experience. Yet you made her feel ashamed of you."

He lowered his hands. His eyes looked hard. "Perhaps we can agree on one more point. As Rachel said, all of you will not fit into my office."

Rachel gasped, as if surprised that Principal Bates had heard her after all.

"I will add my thoughts to Rachel's," he said. "I do not believe the Junction City Skating Rink has room for you, either. You will not be taking part in the scrap metal contest."

Over a rise of complaints, Mark shouted, "We brought in more than anybody!"

"Miss Stewart!" Rachel wailed.

Mark exclaimed, "It was Jap stuff that got broken."

"Not all of it." Was that Christopher? Macy almost turned to look.

Principal Bates had walked to the door. He turned back. "This is not your teacher's decision. The decision is mine and not open to argument."

As soon as the door closed after him, Rachel shoved Macy's shoulder. "It's your fault!"

"Rachel," Miss Stewart snapped. "There is an empty chair in the back. Take it."

"Take it where?" Rachel muttered as the teacher asked Lily to pass out papers for a geography test. Miss Stewart ignored the question.

When Macy walked into the hallway for recess, she noticed Christopher Adams leaning against the opposite wall. Memory flashed. He looked the same way he had on Pearl Harbor day, when he'd broken her necklace and they were both sent to Principal Bates.

He straightened as she came near. "Rachel's outside waiting for you."

"Why?"

"No skating party."

"That's not my fault." Hurt and anger boiled

through Macy. Even Christopher was ordering her around as if he had the right. Clutching the tiny *kokeshi* doll on its chain inside her blouse, she walked past him and down the front stairs.

At the bottom, Rachel greeted her with a surprisingly sympathetic smile. "I shouldn't have shoved you, Macy. I was mad at Principal Bates and I couldn't shove him." She laughed a little. "Amy and I are sharing a cola on a bench beside the stairs. Come and join us."

Macy looked at her, wondering if the invitation was a trick. If she agreed to share the cola, would Rachel shout, *Not with a Jap lover!* and run off?

But maybe Rachel was sorry for the way she had acted. Rachel was a leader. If she was nice, others would be, too.

Macy hesitated just a moment longer before letting Rachel tug her toward a bench placed in a darker area where the stairs met the school wall.

The moment the dark shade closed over her, doubt grew too strong to ignore. Macy turned around. "I'm going to find Lily."

"No. You're not." The laughter was gone. Rachel's voice sounded hard.

Macy looked at her. "I'm not afraid of you, Rachel. If you have something to say to me, say it."

"It's not just me." Rachel sounded smug now, the way a spider might sound once it caught a fly in its web.

Behind Macy, someone shouted, "Grab her!" She recognized Mark's voice as both her arms were caught behind her. Someone hauled her backward, closer to the school wall.

"Let me go!" Macy yelled. "I didn't do anything to you!"

"Shut up!" Rachel's hand whipped around before Macy could duck and smacked hard against the side of her face. "Go live in Japan, Jap lover," she said.

Macy tasted blood and heard taunts. "Don't take that," a boy said to Macy. "Go on, hit her back. Don't you want to?"

They were ready for her to go after Rachel and still held her arms. Instead, she kicked backward. Her foot smacked into a knee. She heard a grunt and felt one of her arms come free.

Swinging around, she punched Mark in the stomach.

As Macy whirled toward Rachel, the other girl shrieked and leaped out of range. Two boys grabbed Macy again. Using the force of her own rush toward Rachel, they swung her around and into the wall. Her head slammed against the wood. As she moaned, one of them punched her face. Her knees buckled, but they held her arms, not letting her fall.

"We don't want you here," one of the boys said in a snarl.

"Get out of our school." Another punched her in the stomach.

She heard running feet. A teacher yelled, "What's going on here?"

Suddenly, Macy was free, falling to the ground while the group scattered in all directions. Miss Stewart rushed to her. "Macy? Oh, my heaven!"

As the teacher knelt beside her, Macy turned her head to spit out blood. At least no teeth came with it.

"Can you stand?" the teacher asked. "We need to get you inside."

She must have looked around. Was there an audience? Miss Stewart called, "Someone, give me a hand. Christopher? Help me with Macy."

Macy wanted to say *Not him*, but the words came out as a moan. A distant part of her memory told her that Christopher wasn't part of it, that he'd tried to warn her away. Maybe he had brought the teacher. She hurt too much to think about it now.

She struggled to her feet while the two of them helped. She felt groggy and her stomach ached. So did her face. Worse was an acid sense of betrayal.

Christopher and Miss Stewart helped her up the stairs and to the nurse's office just past the one for Principal Bates.

"My papa?" Macy asked, wondering if her mouth was swelling.

"Principal Bates will call him," the nurse assured her as she helped her sit on a narrow cot. "Lift your head, hon. I'll just clean away the blood so I can see what we need to do."

When Papa came in minutes later, Macy jumped from the cot and rushed to wrap her arms about his middle. "I didn't cry," she said. "Not once."

She felt his entire body vibrate with anger as he held her for one long moment. Setting her back, he studied her more closely. His eyes narrowed and his mouth looked tight. "Stay here."

As the nurse drew her to sit on the cot again, Macy listened to Papa's hard footsteps stride into the hall and next door into Principal Bates's office. He didn't bother to knock.

CHAPTER 21

Macy couldn't sit still on the narrow bed. She crossed and uncrossed her ankles. She accepted an aspirin and a paper cup filled with water from the nurse, then explored the bruises on her face with her fingertips. All the while, a sense of unfairness swelled inside her.

Why did she have to wait here? She wanted to be with Papa. The men were in there talking about her. In Japan, girls didn't speak out much, but if Miss Tokyo were here, Macy was sure she would say that Macy should hear what the men were saying. Miss Tokyo would be right.

The telephone rang on the far corner of the desk. When the nurse turned away to answer, Macy scooted backward on the cot, closer to the wall, then a little closer.

Another scoot and she heard the men's voices next door. They were muffled, but when she turned her ear to the wall, she could understand their words. Principal Bates was saying nice things about her. "Macy is a bright girl, honest and hardworking." There was a pause. Then he said, "I'm afraid she's blinded by her love for that Japanese doll."

Blinded? What did that mean?

Papa was agreeing, saying he'd been concerned for some time.

There was a pause, and Macy pictured Principal Bates putting his fingertips together, as if that helped him prepare for what he wanted to say next. He'd done that when she was in his office with Christopher, last December.

Macy glanced at the nurse, who was still talking on the telephone, then pressed her ear against the wall so she could hear the men more clearly.

"You aren't able to protect her," Papa said. "I'm going to withdraw her from your school."

Withdraw her!

Sounding regretful, the principal said, "I'm afraid the Japanese doll will always stand in her way with others. For her own safety, she should put the doll out of her mind."

The nurse said quietly to Macy, "Dear, please lie down and rest. Your father will be with you soon."

Macy lay flat, with thoughts whirling in her head. A new school! Where? What about her friends? She wouldn't know anyone. What about Lily?

Moments later, Papa came from the principal's office. Macy scrambled to her feet. "Papa, I won't talk about Miss Tokyo anymore. Please don't make me leave my school!"

His brown eyes looked troubled as he took her hands in his. Quietly, he said, "When I thought you were safely at home, you were chasing the men who wanted to burn Miss Tokyo."

"I saved her, Papa."

"What you did was dangerous. And now this!"

She was afraid to say anything. Sobs threatened to climb up her throat. She tried hard to keep them back.

Papa urged her toward the door. "We'll talk more at home."

• • •

The pastor from their church came by after supper. Macy realized that Papa must have called him. Macy served coffee in the parlor, carefully balancing two full cups on a tray, trying hard to prove to Papa that he needed her with him.

When she came into the parlor, she heard Pastor Wells saying, "You're right, Mr. James. This is not the time to pile more on Macy's young shoulders. This latest news could be too much for her. And remember, there's always hope."

Macy paused, trying to make sense of the words, but the pastor changed the subject to echo Principal Bates's praise. "Macy is a good girl and sharp as a tack. She deserves a fresh start."

Pastor Wells looked up as Macy put the tray on the long mahogany coffee table. She had polished the table just before he arrived, and the gleam of the dark wood made her feel proud. But his words worried her. Were they keeping something from her? Should she ask?

Papa's eyes were already set on the future. "We've placed Miss Tokyo in her original box in the storeroom for safekeeping. There's no longer need to defy the town. With the Stanby's doors locked for inventory, no one will see the doll anyway."

Macy sank into a chair as she remembered carrying the little lamps, tea sets, and all the rest into the storage room in the basement. Miss Tokyo had reassured her, with her pretend voice hushed because of the box, "I will sleep, Macy-chan, until you come for me."

The pastor patted her hand, bringing her thoughts back to the parlor. "Macy, you lived at the coast before you came here. Were you happy there?"

"I liked the beach," Macy said with caution.

"I don't believe either of you met the Farrells, Emory and Ida? They were solid members of our church until five years ago, when they moved to Rockaway, over on the coast."

He looked at Papa, who said slowly, "I met them when they came for the church picnic last summer. Emory, especially, impressed me."

"He's a solid patriot," the pastor said. "He didn't feel he was doing his part for the war effort as the town barber. He signed on as a volunteer air raid warden as soon as FDR created the job. Ida helps with the Red Cross, rolling bandages and whatever. They'll be great examples for Macy."

"Do you think they'll have time for her?"

Macy jerked her attention from the pastor to Papa, then back, as Pastor Wells said, "I talked with them by telephone before coming over. They've both invited Macy into their home until things settle down here."

"That might not be until the war ends." Papa hesitated, not meeting the anguished looks Macy was sending him. "There's talk of the Japanese planning to invade our beaches. I wouldn't want my daughter there if——"

Was there hope? Would Papa change his mind because of danger at the beach?

The pastor's reassurance cut off Papa's fears. "Emory tells me they have people watching every mile of coastline. There won't be any surprise invasion of the Oregon beaches."

Her entire future was being decided for her! Macy reached for Papa's sleeve. "Please, Papa. I don't want to go away. I want to stay here and help you."

"I can't keep you safe." He looked into her eyes, his gaze troubled. For a moment, she thought he might waver. "With Miss Rasmussen gone, there's no one but me to watch over you. Obviously, I've done a poor job."

"No, Papa," she said. "It's my fault. I promise I'll change."

"You need a woman to care for you," Papa said. "You may not think so now, but you'll be happier with the Farrells. And you've always enjoyed the beach. You'll find agates and crazy-looking pieces of driftwood, maybe even glass floats lost from fishermen's nets all the way across the ocean."

"But who will help inventory the museum's collection? And make supper?" Tears brimmed in Macy's eyes. "I don't do as well as Miss Rasmussen, but I'm learning, Papa. I am!" Another question nearly sent the tears spilling over. *If I go away, who will watch over Miss Tokyo?*

"You're doing fine with cooking and the rest, honey," Papa said, surprising her. "But right now, it's better for you to live with the Farrells. I know you'll be a big help."

"Of course she will," the pastor agreed. "Emory told me he's put in a big Victory Garden. Growing vegetables is a good way to help the war effort and work off whatever's bothering you. I'll just bet you'd be good at gardening, Macy."

He looked as if he expected her to smile. She felt as if she might never smile again.

Deep inside, a plan was forming. She would go to the beach and live with strangers. But she wasn't leaving Miss Tokyo here where someone might take her out and burn her. Miss Tokyo was going to live with the Farrells, too. With luck, they would never know she was there.

CHAPTER 22

I'm going to miss you something awful," Lily said on Sunday as she picked at a loose thread on Macy's bedspread.

Macy studied the pile of dresses she had laid out beside Lily. "I wish I knew how long I'll be gone. Maybe I won't need all these."

"You'll be back soon," Lily told her. "The war can't last much longer."

Macy thought she might be wrong. The radio news accounts and the terrible stories in the papers made it sound like the war would never end. "Papa says I do things without talking them over with him, but what's the point of talking when I already know his answer?"

Lily looked confused. "He won't care how many dresses you pack. Will he?"

"No." Macy hesitated, wondering how much to confide in Lily. "I was thinking of Miss Tokyo, of asking to take her with me."

Lily looked at her with the clear light of honesty shining from her eyes. "You can't take her. She's museum property, not yours."

"I want her to be safe."

"She won't be. As soon as you leave, men will burn or bury her. There's nothing you can do, Macy. That doll just gets you into trouble. Tell her good-bye. You have to, Macy. You know that."

Macy wrestled with her conscience. The men who hated Miss Tokyo would be criminals for destroying city property if they burned her. By removing the doll, she'd be saving them from jail!

"You have a funny look on your face," Lily said. "You're not still thinking about taking the doll?"

"I dreamed last night," Macy answered softly. "People were standing around in a circle shouting, 'Burn! Burn!' When I got closer, I saw the bonfire with Miss Tokyo on top. I felt something wet hit my hand and looked up. There was Mama, watching from the clouds. Tears fell from her eyes like rain, splashing the bonfire, but they couldn't stop Miss Tokyo from burning."

"That's your mind telling you that you can't save the doll," Lily said in her most practical voice. "You have to forget about her, Macy. She doesn't matter to your mama anymore. She's passed on. And your father is curator. He can't remove anything from the museum, even if it is in danger."

"He could . . ." *If he was loaning it for a display somewhere.* Lily was her best friend, but Lily's honesty might push her to say more than she should to Papa. So she said only to herself, *I'm going to take Miss Tokyo where I can keep her safe until I can bring her back.*

Lily helped her pack for a long stay away, then hugged her as fiercely as if she never expected to see her again. "Write to me! Promise!"

"I promise. You write to me, too."

"I will!" After another tearful hug, Lily ran down the stairs that to Macy already felt almost alien, as if they had never been part of her life. She forced herself to finish packing before carrying a blanket down and leaving it at the bottom.

She was making sandwiches to take with them on the drive to the coast when the telephone rang in the next room. Papa left to answer. Macy grabbed the blanket from the stairs, paused to be sure Papa was still talking on the phone, then dashed across to the museum storeroom.

For once, she didn't speak to Miss Tokyo, just hauled the packing box toward her, pushed open the lid, and lifted out the doll. Moving quickly, she shoved the box back into place on its lower shelf. She rolled the blanket around the doll, her heart pounding so loudly in her ears she wondered if she would hear Papa if he did come into the museum.

She grabbed Mama's journal from the shelf where she kept it. Since storing Miss Tokyo, Macy had been writing all her notes to Mama while down here visiting the doll in her box. There would be a lot to write about now.

She shoved the journal into her skirt pocket.

Papa mustn't find her here. She couldn't even imagine how upset he would be, but she knew Miss Tokyo would be lost if she went to the beach without her. *I'm doing the right thing, Mama,* she said silently. *I know you agree. I can feel it.*

With the doll in the blanket balanced against her shoulder, she hurried up the stairs and out the back door of the museum to the car. There was no room in the trunk for Miss Tokyo. Papa would be bringing her two big suitcases. Besides, he might discover the doll when he put the suitcases in.

The backseat, then.

She shifted the doll to one arm and struggled to open the car door.

Papa shouted from the porch, "They'll have blankets. You don't need to take your own. It's not a camping trip."

"I'm used to mine," Macy called. "I'll sleep better with my blanket from home."

"I understand." Sadness crossed Papa's face. She thought he was going to say something more, but he simply shook his head before coming over and opening the rear door to the car. "Looks like you're taking your pillow, too."

"I'm used to my pillow." That wasn't a lie. She was used to her pillow. She would miss it, but she wasn't taking it.

"Put them across the seat," he said. "Here, I'll do it."

"I can do it." Quickly, she leaned into the car with the blanketed doll. As she hoisted it in, she lost her balance and nearly fell into the car.

The bundle dropped from her hands onto the

seat. A corner of the blanket fell open. A patch of blue silk gleamed in the dim light.

Macy jerked the blanket into place. Her entire body tensed. Papa might have seen the kimono. She braced inwardly, waiting for him to shout at her to put the doll back.

CHAPTER 23

From across the street, their neighbor Mrs. Randolph called, "Mr. James!"

Macy sensed Papa stepping back and turning away. Relief crashed through her. She grasped the door frame to keep from falling into the car after all.

"You have a bit of a drive ahead," Mrs. Randolph said, hurrying closer. "I've brought some molasses cookies still warm from my oven. They'll give you something to munch on during the trip."

"That's kind of you," Papa said. He looked at Macy as if waiting for her to thank their neighbor.

Macy's thoughts were in the car with the doll, spinning from fear to relief and back again. For a moment, her mind went blank. The good smell rising from the bag with a promise of warm cookies reminded her to smile at Mrs. Randolph. "Yes, thank you. I love your molasses cookies!"

The neighbor patted Macy's shoulder. "You drive safely now, you two. You'll be missed around here, Macy. Never think you won't be."

Macy hugged her, feeling her eyes getting teary. It was easy to forget that most people were nice while you worried about the ones who weren't. She was glad Mrs. Randolph had reminded her.

A boy's voice called from the street, "Got an extra cookie in there?"

Macy let Mrs. Randolph go, surprised to see Christopher Adams. He shoved his hands into his back pockets. "Some of us are going to miss you at school."

She wanted to ask who "some of us" were but suspected it was only Lily. Maybe Christopher. She still wasn't sure she could trust him. She glanced around for Rachel or Mark.

Papa said, "We need to get started."

"Well, good-bye," Macy told Christopher. On impulse, she grabbed a cookie from the bag and handed it to him.

"Yeah." He held the cookie without tasting it

while she climbed into the car, then called, "That was brave, guarding the doll that day we all came to the museum. Dumb. But brave."

Macy stuck out her tongue at him as Papa started the engine. Then she remembered doing the same thing last Christmas. A snowflake had landed on her tongue. She couldn't help smiling at the memory and saw Christopher grin as the car pulled away.

Like the Cheshire Cat, she told herself, but with a quick inner warning. *The Cheshire Cat wasn't always a friend to Alice in Wonderland.*

She was more worried about Miss Tokyo. As Papa's Plymouth rode smoothly past the flat valley and into rolling hills where clumps of mistletoe clung to bare tree branches like forgotten bouquets, Macy struggled with her conscience.

What else could I do? she demanded of herself as the road climbed through the Coast Range, where the trees had green needles year-round. Moss-covered fallen logs and thick green ferns hid the forest floor.

Miss Tokyo would be burned if I left her in the museum. Lily's right. Men are planning to come for the doll.

Macy resisted peering over the seat to the

blanket that covered Miss Tokyo. *Call her Miss T,* she told herself. *She'll be safer if I forget and mention her if I just call her Miss T. Everybody hates Tokyo right now.*

She felt as if Mama spoke in her gentle voice. *You've done the right thing, love,* she was saying. *You must keep Miss Tokyo safe.*

"I will." Macy pressed the journal through her pocket. "I always will." Turning, she gazed through the car window at light rain falling over the dark damp forest and thought of her dream, where Mama's tears from heaven could not save the doll from a bonfire.

But I will save her. For the moment, at least, her conscience was silent. She had done what she had to do. Papa would understand. But she couldn't tell him, not just yet.

As they came down from the Coast Range into flat dairy country, Macy's attention was caught by construction at the back of a field. Men were building a structure bigger than any barn she had ever seen. The men looked about the size of ants. Even their equipment looked like toys against the enormous structure. "What are they building, Papa?"

He said quietly, "That's a blimp hangar."

"A blimp?" The pastor had mentioned that word.

"An airship," Papa said. "Like an enormous oval balloon. You've heard of zeppelins? A cabin attached below holds the pilot and crew. That hangar will shelter as many as eight of the ships."

"Why?" She turned in her seat to look back at the blimp hangar.

Papa didn't answer at first. When she looked at him, she saw that his expression was as tight as when war news came over the radio, news he wanted to hear but didn't think she should know. Papa thought that knowing about blimps would worry her.

He must have decided she would learn anyway, because he did answer. "The blimps will patrol the coast. They'll fly above the surf . . . to keep us safe."

Safe? He meant safe from submarines. The men who flew in the cabins beneath the blimps would be looking for Japanese submarines bringing the war to beaches here. Suddenly, the war felt even scarier than when it was just news over the radio.

"Don't worry about it," Papa said with a glance toward her. "The blimp hangars and the activity you'll see around the Coast Guard headquarters farther up the coast at Garibaldi are there for protection. You should feel safe because the brave men of our country are alert for trouble and ready to defend us if necessary."

Macy wanted to feel comforted, the way she used to feel when Papa looked into the closet and joked about shooing away a monster who only wanted a peek at a human child.

This monster might not be shooed away so easily. She thought of Miss Tokyo, riding along in the backseat. It rained a lot at the coast. Maybe a bonfire to burn an enemy doll would fizzle out.

As the miles rolled on, Macy wasn't soothed by the warm car or by the wipers whipping back and forth or even by Papa beside her. The closer she got to the small beach town called Rockaway, only twenty miles north of Tillamook, the less bringing Miss Tokyo felt like a rescue. Now it felt like an impossible responsibility, one Macy was beginning to think she should never have taken on.

The few cars on the road had the top halves of their headlights blacked out so their light would go down but not forward. Macy wondered if that would keep a submarine from noticing a highway along the coast.

After passing the Coast Guard station and traveling over a rocky headland, Macy could hear waves crashing onto rocks. A little farther out and even in the rainy dark, she could see the white line of breakers crashing over and rolling onto the sand.

I'm going to live with nice people, she assured herself. *Pastor wouldn't send me to them unless they were kind. They probably like dolls. They'll understand that a doll had nothing to do with the war. I'll be able to tell them how Mama and I talked for Miss Tokyo and shared the pictures in Mama's big book.*

Macy was so caught up in her thoughts, she barely noticed several tiny beach towns, one after another, until Papa turned off the highway and down a long graveled road with trees along one side and a flat darkness that might have been a field or a garden on the other.

After turning to the right, Papa parked beside a gate.

"The Farrells aren't expecting us," Macy said, looking through the car window at the dark bulk of a house at the end of a gravel walkway. "Maybe they've already gone to bed."

"They've closed the blackout curtains," Papa explained, opening the car door. "The curtains are used every night here, not just for drills."

"Oh." Macy's voice sounded much smaller than the hammer of rain pelting the roof of the car. If only Papa would turn them around and drive right back to Stanby. He wouldn't. She was here and had to stay, but she had hoped for a warm welcoming hug, not this silent dark house looming two stories high against the deepening night. The chimney didn't even show sparks with the promise of a warm fire in the stove below.

CHAPTER 24

Papa knocked hard on the door. "Emory?"

The door opened a crack, then wider, revealing a stern face. "Come in, quickly. We can't let out any more light than we have to. The blackout, you know."

"We know, Emory. We have drills in the valley." Papa urged Macy into the house with a hand on her shoulder, though she wanted to run back to the car. He added to the man who held the door barely wide enough for them to pass, "Your neighbor must not have gotten that message."

The man named Emory leaned out to look across the road at a small house where light slanted from the corner of a window. To Macy, it looked as if the blackout curtain had gotten hung up on something.

"That old fool," Emory exclaimed. "Sometimes I wonder if old Mr. Oakes hopes to guide the whole Jap navy to us." After grabbing a baton from somewhere to his left, he rushed toward his neighbor's house.

Moments later, they heard his baton rapping against the neighbor's window. "Lights out!" he shouted. "Lights out!"

Macy shivered and thought again of running back to the warm, friendly car.

Before she could plead with Papa, a woman came through the dimly lit interior of the big house and took Macy's cold hands in her warm ones. "Never mind, dear. Mr. Farrell takes his duties as air raid warden very seriously. As he should."

She turned to Papa. "Our neighbor across the street is the burden we have to shoulder. The poor old fellow can't seem to remember to check his curtains after closing them."

"People have trouble believing enemy troops will come here," Papa said. Macy felt his quick glance, as if wanting to reassure her before he added, "Who can blame them? Our armed forces are on guard."

"And Mr. Farrell," Macy couldn't resist saying.

Papa's hand tightened over her shoulder in warning, but Mrs. Farrell smiled. "She has a sense of humor. Lovely. We need some laughter around here."

She glanced down at Macy's hands. "Goodness, child, you feel half frozen. Come in by the fire and warm yourself."

When Macy started into the house, one foot banged so painfully into solid metal she felt as if stars flew up from her toes. Gasping, she stumbled forward.

"Oh dear, that's our sand bucket." Mrs. Farrell's voice filled with apology. "You'll get used to low lighting. Even with the curtains, we don't risk keeping the rooms any brighter than necessary."

"Sand?" Macy could feel grains beneath her feet, gritty on the linoleum floor. She must have knocked them from the bucket, but who kept sand in the house?

She tried to imagine the Farrells playing in sand—maybe building castles. No, that image matched Mama, not the people here.

Mrs. Farrell explained. "Along the coast, we all keep sand by the door these days. "We'll use it to put out fires caused by bombs when . . . if . . . enemy planes get through."

She reached behind the door for a broom and dustpan. Looking as if she'd had a lot of practice, she swept up the spilled grains and dumped them back into the bucket.

"Keeping sand off the floor and in the bucket can be a little job for you while you're with us, dear."

"Okay." Macy felt as if she'd walked into a strange world where she didn't belong and didn't want to be. She couldn't stay here until the war ended.

Mrs. Farrell led her to a potbellied woodstove with a low fire burning inside. No revealing sparks would be escaping up this chimney, Macy told herself, remembering the dark chimney against the sky. She held her hands near the cast iron, trying to warm them.

The front door cracked open and Mr. Farrell slipped through. "That old fool will guide the bombers right to us. Some folks are wondering if that's his plan."

"Oh, not old Del," Mrs. Farrell exclaimed. "He has a good heart. You know he does, dear. He's just at a forgetful age."

"If he doesn't keep his blackout curtains closed, the rest of us may not have the chance to reach that age," her husband warned.

These were the kind people Pastor Wells had chosen for her? Macy looked from one to the other. Mrs. Farrell seemed nice, but Mr. Farrell . . . To use their words about their neighbor, Mr. Farrell was going to be a burden she would have to shoulder. She glanced at Papa, wishing she could share that thought but knowing he wouldn't appreciate it.

"We just have to keep our eye on his place a little longer," Mrs. Farrell was explaining. "Mr. Oakes says his niece wants him to come to the valley to live with them, but he won't budge. So she's sending her boy — Cee-Cee, they call him — out to check on his great-uncle's curtains and keep his bucket filled with sand."

"You'll have company," Papa said to Macy. Silently, she told herself she wouldn't be around long enough to meet the nephew.

"Papa, I should go home with you and make sure all our curtains are closed tightly every night."

Mr. Farrell chuckled, sounding friendlier. "Your Papa knows the danger as well as I do. Nobody needs to worry about us following the rules."

Mrs. Farrell put one hand on her husband's arm, smiling at him in a proud way. "Emory's doing everything he can to keep us safe. He even took all the glass floats I'd found on the beach over the years and shot them. They floated here from Japan, you know."

Macy swallowed a laugh. Maybe she was over-tired, but she wanted to giggle at a mental image of glass balls lined up for targets with cartoon-style faces painted on them. No, he probably painted red suns on them and pretended the floats were Japanese planes.

To keep the thought to herself, she asked seriously, "But didn't the floats break loose from fishing nets long before the war? It must have taken years for them to drift all this way. Why shoot them?"

"They look innocent," Mr. Farrell said. "Thinking that way is the kind of mistake the Japs hope we'll make. Those people plan way ahead, little miss. Any one of those floats might have been hiding a bomb."

There was no humor in Macy now. Her last hope for Miss Tokyo drained away. If Mr. Farrell saw bombs in harmless fishing floats, he wasn't going to have kind thoughts for a Japanese doll. Somehow, she would have to keep the doll hidden the entire time she stayed here.

First, she had to get Miss Tokyo from the car. "I brought my blanket from home," she said, adding quickly, "I'll sleep better with it over me."

Mr. Farrell frowned. "Most little girls grow out of needing a favorite blanket before they're your age."

Papa surprised Macy by saying, "It's a harmless comfort. I'll bring it in."

"I'll get it, Papa." Macy rushed for the door, remembering to open it just a crack before slipping through.

Outside, with rain falling and clouds making the night even darker, she moved carefully, feeling her way along the walk to the gate. The car loomed in the darkness. When she opened the back door into the familiar interior, still warm with the scent of home, tears nearly choked her.

She wiped her cheeks with her damp coat sleeve before reaching into the car. After a bit of fumbling, she located the bundle with Miss Tokyo inside. She made sure the doll was completely covered by the blanket before she carried it to the house.

Papa and the Farrells stood around the warm stove. They looked as if they'd been talking about something she shouldn't hear and had stopped almost but not quite in time. She had heard disapproval in Mr. Farrell's voice when he asked Papa, "When will you tell Macy?"

She stopped just inside the door after making sure it was closed, wanting to ask, *Tell me what?* She bit the words back. She would wait until she was alone with Papa. "May I put this on my bed?"

"You'll be sleeping upstairs." Mr. Farrell took the two suitcases Papa had set on the floor and walked ahead of Macy into a hall and up a narrow staircase. Macy held the bundle more tightly. All the way up the stairs after Mr. Farrell, she pictured him discovering Miss Tokyo and whipping out his gun.

Mr. Farrell opened the door on the left of a narrow landing and, after checking the window curtain, turned on a small lamp. The room she would be using was under the eaves, with the ceiling starting low on each side and sloping up to a peak in the center. Flowered wallpaper kept the wind from coming through any cracks.

Beds stood against each wall. Macy warned

herself not to sit up suddenly and knock her head on the low ceiling.

Mr. Farrell nodded at the bundle clutched in her arms. "Do you need help with that?"

"No!" Then she added with the warmest smile she could manage, "Thank you, Mr. Farrell."

The moment he left her alone in the room, she slipped the doll and the roll of blanket beneath the bed, pushing them as far toward the wall as she could. "I'm sorry, Miss Tokyo, but you have to hide."

Mrs. Farrell had looked to her like a careful housekeeper who would make sure to sweep beneath every bed. This would not be a safe hiding place for long.

In her mind, Mama was looking down at the doll and wringing her hands with worry. "It will be all right," Macy promised both the doll and Mama. "I'll look for a better place tomorrow."

When she hurried downstairs, dinner was on the big table at the kitchen end of the front room. She felt hunger rumble in her stomach and was glad to slip onto a wooden chair.

By the time they'd finished a bowl of thick onion-and-potato chowder with tender homemade biscuits, the Farrells were yawning. "We're used to early bedtime around here," Mr. Farrell said.

Mrs. Farrell rose from the table. "You and your father will be sleeping upstairs, dear. Come along now and help me hang a blanket down the middle of the room to give you both your privacy. Shall we use the special blanket you brought with you?"

CHAPTER 25

No!" Macy would have clutched the blanket and Miss T close, but they were upstairs under the bed. "It's . . . not big enough."

"It's not?" Mrs. Farrell's eyebrows rose. "It looked hefty when you carried it in."

Macy stood as if frozen while thoughts rushed through her head, none of them answers for Mrs. Farrell. At any moment, Mr. Farrell would demand to see the blanket and everything would be ruined. Why hadn't she thought to hide the doll in the museum, maybe in the sarcophagus with the mummy? But the lid was so heavy. And the mummy would be dusty. . . .

She saw Mrs. Farrell's expression become gentle. "I understand," the woman said. "The blanket is a bit of home. You want it warm beneath your cheek, not hanging out in the cold."

Macy nodded, daring to hope her secret would still be safe.

"You're exhausted, poor child." Mrs. Farrell patted Macy's shoulder. "The bathroom is off the kitchen. I've left a clean washcloth beside the basin and a toothbrush in case you forgot to bring one. Go ahead and wash up. I'll have an extra blanket hung up for a curtain by the time you're ready to climb into bed."

Macy hurried through her preparations, then rushed up the stairs. Relief made her knees wobble when she saw that Mrs. Farrell was just finishing pinning a pink cotton blanket to a clothesline stretched from the middle of the window to the middle of the upper door frame.

"We each have our own little room now," Macy said, and impulsively hugged the woman. "Thank you, Mrs. Farrell."

Mrs. Farrell hugged her back. "You're very welcome, dear. Say your prayers and hop into bed. You'll be starting school tomorrow, so that will be another busy day for you."

Once into her nightgown and alone upstairs, Macy scrambled across her bed and peered into the dark crack next to the wall. "Good night," she whispered. "Don't worry, Miss T. I'll keep you safe, I promise."

Papa came up the stairs a little later. Macy called a soft good-night as the bedsprings beyond the hanging blanket squeaked beneath his weight. Rain drumming on the roof lulled her to sleep far more quickly than she expected.

She woke early, sitting straight up, calling, "Mama!"

It took a moment to realize she had been dreaming. In the dream, Mama was trapped under her wheelchair and calling for her. That was dumb. Mama was safe in heaven. She wasn't trapped and she didn't need the wheelchair anymore.

Even so, Macy slid closer to the wall and slipped her hand down to feel the familiar bulk of the Japanese doll wrapped in the blanket. "Mama's safe, Miss T. We just have to get used to this new place."

From the doorway, Mrs. Farrell said, "Do you have an imaginary friend, dear? Someone named Misty?"

Macy squirmed upright. "No, I don't . . ." She

trailed off. Mrs. Farrell hadn't guessed about the doll. Wasn't it better for her to think there was an invisible playmate, even though that was something a younger girl would have?

Mrs. Farrell smiled. "Misty is more of a name for a puppy, but I suppose since she's invisible, it doesn't matter what your friend is called."

Macy looked toward the other bed. The curtain between them was pulled back to the window, and the blankets were folded neatly at the foot. A dream-like memory came back to her of Papa coming in very early to kiss her forehead and say good-bye. He'd said something else. She frowned, thinking hard. That he would be in touch. That was it. He'd left her with a promise, one she would cling to.

"Your papa wanted you to rest this morning," Mrs. Farrell said, "but we'll need to get you into school before the first bell rings. Mr. Farrell will drive you over on his way to work. Breakfast is waiting downstairs."

Macy mentally winced at the thought of a new school, a school where she was expected to start over and never talk about Miss Tokyo. "Papa can drive me."

"He left at daybreak, dear. He wanted to get

an early start back to the valley. Do you need help with your clothes?"

"No. I'll be right down." She heard more in her voice, and based on the worried furrow over Mrs. Farrell's eyes, she'd heard it, too: a silent wail. *I'm left here with people I don't know. When will Papa come back for me?*

Why hadn't she asked him? But she'd been so sleepy she barely remembered his telling her good-bye.

We all have to do our part for the war. She remembered Miss Rasmussen saying that before she left to join the WAACS. *My part is to keep Miss Tokyo safe for the kids who will visit her in the museum someday,* Macy decided, *and that means staying here for now.*

As Mrs. Farrell walked down the stairs, Macy pulled the journal from under her pillow. She needed to find a safe place to keep it. For now, in case Mrs. Farrell accidentally saw the last entries, she wrote carefully, *Dear Mama, it's nice to be at the beach again. From my bedroom, I can hear the rumble of the waves. The Farrells are very kind.*

After tucking the journal away, Macy slid out from under the warm patchwork quilt and padded over a thin rug to the window. She looked out on a freshly rainwashed world. To the north, a small lake gleamed blue beyond a fringe of willow trees.

The double windows opened outward. When she leaned through them to look west, she could see over low trees all the way to the roofs of cottages on the rise of the dune between the highway and the sand.

The beach was so near, the ocean sounded even louder. She could *smell* it. How soon could she explore? After school?

A man came from the small cottage across the road. The collar was turned up on a long black coat that hung almost to his ankles. Despite the coat, he looked cold. When he walked along the road, Macy heard the jingle of small bells.

She looked more closely. The man wore a striped knit cap with little bells tied into a tassel on the top. "Old Mr. Oakes," she breathed. That's who he was, old Mr. Oakes who wasn't careful enough with his blackout curtains. But what a funny cap for an old man!

Mr. Farrell had said people were beginning to think Mr. Oakes let light gleam past his blackout curtains on purpose. She knew — she wasn't sure how, but she knew — they were wrong. Old Mr. Oakes was not a traitor. "He's not a spy," she said aloud, turning toward Miss Tokyo under the bed. "People don't trust him and it isn't fair. I think Mr. Oakes is a lot like me."

When she slipped into place at the large table at the far end of the front room, a big bowl of crunchy cereal was already waiting. As Mrs. Farrell poured milk into the bowl, she asked, "Have you eaten puffed rice before?"

Macy scooped her spoon beneath several of the puffs. "Rice?"

Mr. Farrell sat at the head of the table with a plate full of bacon and eggs, but his attention was on a stand nearby and a big square box with a lot of tubes and dials. He twisted a dial past a burst of radio static as he glanced at Macy. "They shoot the rice from guns to get it puffed like that."

"Guns?" Macy looked at the rice in her bowl. How did that work?

Mrs. Farrell chuckled. "That's their motto—rice shot from guns—but I doubt they mean the kind of guns our soldiers use. As I understand it, the cereal makers get the rice wet so it will steam when they heat it under pressure. When they release the pressure, the rice pops into these puffs."

"Like popcorn?" Macy tasted the rice and

decided she liked it. "Do they sell it at your grocery store?"

"The Watkins Man stopped by with his van full of spices and such yesterday," Mrs. Farrell explained. "Puffed rice isn't rationed, so I bought a bag. I thought it would be something special to welcome you into our family."

"That was nice of you," Macy said, glad she liked the puffed rice. As she raised another spoonful, she remembered to add, "Thank you, Mrs. Farrell."

"Oh, that's so formal," Mrs. Farrell said quickly. "Why don't you just call me Aunt Ida? I know we're not blood related, but we'll pretend."

"I'd like that," Macy said, meaning it. Maybe living here wouldn't be so awful after all.

A room-shaking burst of static blared from Mr. Farrell's box.

"Mercy!" Mrs. Farrell exclaimed.

Mr. Farrell turned a dial to get past the racket. Macy couldn't help asking, "What kind of radio is that?"

"This is called a shortwave radio," he answered. "Our regular radio announcers just tell us what they think we should hear. With this, I'll hear what people all over the world are saying."

All over the world! Macy marveled at the

thought that voices could travel so far on radio waves, although Mr. Farrell was just getting a lot of awful noise.

She had hoped to meet Mr. Oakes, but after breakfast Mr. Farrell hustled her into his Chevrolet sedan for a ride to school. "You'll be walking after today," he warned when he pulled to a stop in front of a white school with a bell tower. "This is just a mile or so down the highway from the house, not far."

Macy nodded, her attention on the two-story wood building. It didn't look like the school she was used to. Suddenly, she felt the way she had last night when Papa parked the car outside the Farrells' tall dark house.

"Come along," Mr. Farrell said. "You don't want to be late on your first day."

Macy clutched the lunch bag Aunt Ida had handed her and hurried up the walk after him. The school office was just inside the front door. Registration went quickly, but the first bell rang before she'd finished answering questions.

Mr. Farrell had gone by then, leaving her to Mrs. Johansen, a pleasant middle-aged secretary wearing a hand-crocheted sweater over her cotton dress. Once the paperwork was done, the secretary pointed her toward a sixth-grade classroom. "Just go in there, dear. Your teacher's name is Miss Ross. Hand this slip to her."

The empty hallway seemed to stretch longer at both ends than it had when she came in with Mr. Farrell. She wanted to run for the front door, but now it looked far away. Feeling as if moths fluttered inside her chest, she opened the classroom door Mrs. Johansen had indicated and stepped inside. Nearly a dozen students looked up from their desks.

CHAPTER 26

Macy's steps sounded loud on the wood floor as she walked to the teacher and handed her the admission slip. People whispered and stared while Miss Ross read the note.

The teacher rapped her desk for attention. "Class, please say hello to our new student, Macy James."

The entire class replied in singsongy voices, "Hello, Macy James," followed by several giggles and one spitball while Miss Ross was directing Macy to an empty desk.

Worry settled like wave-washed stones in Macy's stomach. She missed Lily. She would even be glad to see Christopher Adams!

A girl at the desk ahead of hers turned around. "I'm Linda." She looked closely at Macy. "When are you going back to your own school?"

Macy wondered if Linda had thrown the spitball. "Not as soon as I want to."

Linda grinned. "Then we might as well be friends."

Macy felt the coldness inside begin to ebb as she smiled back. "Guess we might as well."

Linda added, "I like your necklace."

Macy heard pride in her voice when she answered. "Thanks. My brother sent it to me. He's in the navy."

But she wouldn't tell Linda or anyone else about Miss Tokyo. A tight feeling rippling through her body warned that she had saved the doll from the neighbors in Stanby and brought her somewhere even more dangerous.

No, Macy decided. *Miss Tokyo is not going to be in danger, because from this moment on, they'll call me the most patriotic girl in town.*

She leaned forward to whisper to Linda. "I'm going to start a scrap drive like Little Orphan Annie in the funny papers. Do you want to be one of Annie's Junior Commandos with me?"

Linda swung around again. "Yes! The president says we all have to do our part."

"We'll earn our stripes by collecting scrap," Macy said, remembering more of the president's advice.

Across the aisle, a girl whispered, "Can I do it, too?"

Macy realized that whispers were going all around the room, but this time they sounded friendly. A boy a row over called, "It's not just for girls, you know. Boys can collect scrap, too."

Miss Ross clapped her hands for silence. "Class, please settle down." She nodded at Macy. "A scrap drive is an excellent idea, but please make plans outside of school, not during our history lesson."

The boy behind Macy tugged the back of her hair. "I'm in, too. Don't forget."

She turned long enough to agree. "Everyone's in. Everyone who wants to be."

When she faced the front of the room and opened her new history book, a warm feeling spread through her. This school was going to be all right. She would make it be all right. She just wished Lily were here to help.

Lifting the little silver anchor on its chain, she

made sure to place it in plain sight over her blouse. Her brother was already helping her fit in with the new school.

At recess, only girls gathered around Macy to plan their scrap drive. Then Linda yelled across the ball field to her brother, who was in the seventh grade, one year ahead of them. "Vincent! I have dibs on our wagon after school."

"What? No!" A red-haired boy charged toward Linda. He made Macy think uneasily of Mark back home. A group of Vincent's friends followed, including some Macy recognized from her sixth-grade class. "We're going to use it to collect scrap."

"So are we." Linda planted her feet solidly and knotted her hands on her hips. "And I said dibs first."

"I thought it," Vincent yelled back.

The others — Linda's friends and Vincent's — began shouting, too.

Macy almost expected to be shoved back and forth the way she was on that awful day when her *kokeshi* doll necklace was nearly ruined. "Stop!" she called. "It's for our soldiers! Remember?"

Everyone fell silent. They looked at one another.

Vincent said, "Okay, you can use the wagon first. We'll collect more scrap than you, anyway."

"It's not a contest," Linda said.

"It could be," one of the girls exclaimed. "We can collect more scrap metal than any old boys!"

"Can not!" one of the boys countered.

"Sure, we can," a third girl said. "Those boys will stop to play ball."

"You think so?" Vincent glanced around at his friends. "All right, now it *is* a contest. You can use the wagon first and we'll still beat you."

Miss Ross hurried toward them. "What is all the shouting?" she demanded. "Is there a problem?"

"No, Miss Ross," Macy said. "We're just deciding how to help fight the war." She looked around at her new friends and realized she wasn't missing Lily as much as she had before.

After promising to meet the group later, Macy walked from school to the Farrells' home. Mrs. Farrell approved the idea of a scrap drive but had chores that needed to be done first. "Ladies will be coming over this afternoon to roll bandages for the Red Cross. I'd like you to help. Maybe you'll have time before supper to talk to the nearest neighbors about saving their tin cans."

Macy glanced across the gravel road to Mr. Oakes's small cabin, wondering how many tin cans he used and if he would save the empty ones for her.

"There's an old baby buggy still hanging on the wall in the garage. That should hold a lot of empty cans." Mrs. Farrell smiled and set the teakettle on the top of the iron stove to stay hot.

Half a dozen ladies soon arrived. They were all pleasant to Macy, but impatience burned inside as she rolled strips of cloth cut from old sheets worn soft. Every one of the ladies had already promised her empty cans to someone from school. Both boys and girls must have dashed off to ask their neighbors the moment they got home.

Now as she watched the shadows grow longer, Macy knew she wouldn't have time to talk to anyone about scrap today.

When Mr. Farrell drove home from the barbershop, the sun was setting behind a bank of clouds over the ocean.

Macy held the door as the last of the ladies left, then called, "I'm going to look for that baby buggy, Mrs. Farrell."

"Aunt Ida, dear," the woman corrected gently.

"If the buggy is too high for you to reach, Uncle Emory will help you."

Macy nodded. It was hard to think of them as aunt and uncle. Maybe that would be easier when she knew them better.

"Take your coat," Aunt Ida reminded her. "It's getting cold outside."

Macy shrugged into the cloth coat she'd left on a hook in the hall, thinking she didn't plan to be outside long enough to need it. Supper would be ready in a few minutes.

Rain had begun to fall when she stepped into the garage, which had three sides but no doors. She stood still for a moment, listening to raindrops hitting the galvanized-metal roof overhead. If she were home in Stanby, she could sit by the warm kitchen range while she sipped a cup of hot chocolate.

Thoughts like that weren't helping. Shaking them away, she located the baby buggy, hanging from hooks on one wall. She had to climb onto a box to reach it but managed to lift it down. Dust filtered from the rattan when she moved it. Maybe she should just set it in the rain for a few minutes to get it clean.

As soon as the thought came to her, she pushed the buggy to the open end of the garage and outside into the rain. Across the gravel road, a beam of light shone from under one side of Mr. Oakes's blackout curtain.

CHAPTER 27

Should she tell Mr. Farrell? *Uncle Emory,* she reminded herself, adding, *Why bother when I can just run over there?*

She was glad of a scarf tucked into her coat pocket and pulled it over her hair before running through the light rainfall.

Mr. Oakes answered her knock, his white eyebrows rising in surprise. "You're the young lady from across the street. Macy, isn't it? I've heard them call you that."

"Yes, Macy," she agreed, and pointed past him into the house. "Your curtain caught on something again."

He turned toward his window and shook his head. "Too many books piled everywhere. I suppose Mr. Farrell sent you to scold me."

"No!" Macy exclaimed. "No, I wanted to warn you. I wouldn't like having someone bang on my window and shout at me to turn out my lights."

"That's kindly thinking, young miss, and I thank you." He glanced around the room as if seeing the piled books, magazines, and newspapers through fresh eyes. "And now you're thinking what an awful clutter."

"No," Macy said again, adding from her heart, "To me, it looks like a library where you don't have to be quiet."

He chuckled, sounding surprised and pleased as he crossed to free the offending curtain from books stacked on a windowsill. "A library where you don't have to be quiet. I like the sound of that."

He glanced toward her as he added the books to others piled on the table. "Do you like to read, Miss Macy?"

"Yes. I used to read with my mama before she died, especially her big book with pictures of places in Japan."

Macy clamped her mouth shut, afraid of

betraying Miss Tokyo. What would Mr. Oakes think of a big Japanese doll hidden beneath a bed in the Farrells' house, when the Farrells were such patriotic people?

"Japan is a beautiful country," he said.

"With nice people," Macy agreed, remembering Mama. She added quickly, "Some of them. Others are fighting us." She glanced across the street. "I have to go. Supper's ready and they don't know where I am."

"Thank you for the warning," he called after her. "I'll watch out for that curtain."

She waved, wondering if he could see her in the dark as she ran back across the road. Mr. Oakes was nicer than the Farrells had made her expect. She was glad to have warned him before Mr. Farrell went out with his loud shouts and baton.

In the next few days, the garden demanded Macy's help. Even with winter coming on, there was a lot to do: mostly cleanup to prepare for the Victory Garden that would be there next spring.

At school Macy had little to add when her new friends compared the amounts of scrap they had collected. All she could contribute was what Aunt

Ida was able to find. She hadn't even thought to ask Mr. Oakes for his cans the night she warned him that his curtain was caught again.

Her other nearest neighbors lived much farther up the tree-lined road, almost to the highway. Macy often saw Mr. Oakes walking along the road in his heavy coat and knit cap with bells on top. When she waved, he nodded in a neighborly way, but she didn't have time to talk to him, and he didn't seem inclined to stop.

Every night, Uncle Emory fiddled with his short-wave radio, bringing in voices from faraway places while Macy did her homework across the table. Life had taken on a routine that didn't leave time for Little Orphan Annie's scrap-collecting Junior Commandos.

On Friday, when Macy once again rushed upstairs to change from her school clothes before helping with the garden, she felt her enthusiasm running out like the tide.

She threw herself across her covers to peer between the bed and the wall at Miss Tokyo, bundled below. "Miss T," she said softly, "I don't think I'll have time to collect a single tin can besides the few Aunt Ida can give me."

"Your friends will forgive you, Macy-chan," she answered in the doll's high voice.

"They've all known each other most of their lives," Macy said. "They have close friends already. So they're not really friends to me. Not like Lily. Not even like Christopher Adams."

Why had she thought of him? She wanted to make the doll laugh and say that at least she didn't have him here making fun of her.

Aunt Ida called up the stairs. "Macy?"

"Coming!" Macy scrambled off the bed and hurried down the stairs. She found Aunt Ida in the open garage beside gleaming tools, each hanging from a nail on one wall. The woman took down a freshly sharpened hoe with markings on the handle. "You should be using this to chop out the old corn stalks. It's a good hoe. Mr. Toyama treated his tools well."

Macy took the hoe and turned it to see unusual markings on the handle.

"Uncle Emory doesn't lend them out," Aunt Ida continued, "but you've proved to be a responsible young lady. I don't believe he'll mind if you use this today."

"Who is Mr. Toyama?" Macy asked, realizing that the markings were Japanese characters that spelled a word or a name.

Aunt Ida walked across the driveway toward the

garden. "He was a friend of Uncle Emory's, but he had to go to an internment camp with the others."

Like Betsy Oshima and her family. *But not her dog,* Macy thought. "How did Uncle Emory get his tools?"

"Mr. Toyama won't be using them in the camp," Aunt Ida said briskly. "It wouldn't be helping him any to leave them in his shed, going rusty and dull."

"So you're taking care of them for him?"

"Yes, but I doubt if he'll be coming back here. Now, pull on the gardening gloves. You'll be finished with the corn stalks before you know it."

Macy looked at the dry stalks, all of them leaning in different directions or lying flat on the ground. She set to work using the sharp hoe and was pleased to see that the stalks fell more quickly than she had expected. Silently, she murmured thanks to the Japanese man who had selected and cared for his tools.

Even so, the work seemed to take forever. When she finally reached the end of the garden nearest the road, she thought it must be almost time for Uncle Emory to get home from the barbershop. And then it would be time for supper. And homework. Again.

She hurled a last stalk away from her. "This is not fun!"

"Macy!" Aunt Ida's call made Macy jump while heat rushed to her face. She had the awful feeling she'd been caught sounding like a four-year-old. Aunt Ida came toward her with a covered plate.

"I've made some oatmeal cookies," the woman explained. "Will you take these over to Mr. Oakes? I doubt that man eats much, living alone the way he does."

Macy could smell the cookies even though they were covered. It would be tempting to take them into the trees and eat them all. But they were for Mr. Oakes. Besides, she wanted to talk to the man with bells on his knit cap.

She pulled off the gloves and left them next to the hoe before taking the plate. "I'll bet he eats these. They smell so good, I'll bet he eats them all."

"Come straight back," Aunt Ida said. "Uncle Emory will be home at any minute and then we'll have supper."

Temptation grew as the cookies' spicy aroma swirled around Macy, but she carried the entire plateful to the small cottage across the gravel road. When she knocked, Mr. Oakes came to the door, still wearing his heavy coat hanging loose over a knit sweater and dark pants.

He must feel cold all the time in the windy, damp climate of the coast. She was glad she'd brought the cookies. Maybe the oatmeal and spices would warm him up some.

He looked at the plate and breathed in deeply. "Is that cinnamon I smell? And vanilla. Could those be cookies?"

"They're for you," Macy said. "Mrs. Farrell sent them."

"That is good of her. And it is kindly of you to take the trouble to bring them. I saw you working in the garden over there," he added with sympathy in his voice. "It looked like unpleasant work."

Embarrassed, Macy realized he must have seen her hurl the corn stalk. "It's just that my friends are having a scrap drive," she said. "I wanted to prove I'm as patriotic as they are."

Mr. Oakes's clear-eyed gaze seemed to look right into her. She was almost afraid he saw Miss Tokyo hiding behind her eyes. "It can be hard to be the newcomer," he said. "I remember that."

It was especially hard to be the newcomer with a secret, Macy thought, but she kept that worry to herself. "They decided on a contest to see who gets the most scrap, the girls or the boys. And here I am working in an old garden! It's going to be a Victory Garden, but even that doesn't feel as patriotic as collecting scrap for our soldiers!"

A sparkle came into Mr. Oakes's eyes. "I can help you there. You're welcome to the heap of empty cans piled out behind my place waiting for my grown son to haul them away."

"You have cans? And I can take them?" She was afraid to believe it.

"Why not?" Mr. Oakes asked. "You will get more use out of those cans than my son. He simply hauls them to the dump."

Mr. Oakes didn't look like he'd welcome hugs, so Macy hugged herself instead. "Can I get them right now?" She stopped, remembering. "A boy is coming to live with you. Your nephew? He might be in my class. Will he be mad if you give away the cans?"

"Not if we don't tell him."

Macy giggled. "Okay."

"You bring Emory Farrell's wheelbarrow around and I will help you load."

A wheelbarrow! She hadn't thought of that. It wasn't a wagon, but she would get less teasing with cans in a wheelbarrow than in a baby buggy.

She saw a question in Mr. Oakes's eyes. He was wondering why it mattered so much to her to be the most patriotic, but he didn't ask. She was thankful for that. She liked him, but she couldn't tell him about Miss Tokyo.

"I might have to get the cans tomorrow," she said as Uncle Emory's car came down the road to the house. "I need to ask if I can use the wheelbarrow, and it will be supper time before I can ask, and after supper I have to roll bandages for the Red Cross again and do my homework."

"Whenever you can make it will be fine," Mr. Oakes answered.

Macy hoped so. The way her luck was running and with the Farrells keeping her so busy, that nephew would turn up and claim all the cans for the boys' scrap drive before she could get to them.

CHAPTER 28

Collecting scrap is a worthwhile job for you," Uncle Emory agreed at breakfast on Macy's first Saturday with them. "But I'd like you to finish cleaning the garden. You've done well. You should be able to clear the tomato patch today."

He twisted the dial on his shortwave radio, causing a fresh burst of loud static.

Macy tried not to frown. The other kids were meeting with their scrap again today. She had to remember that the Farrells were being kind in letting her stay here. She had to keep reminding herself of that. The way she had to keep reminding herself to call them Aunt and Uncle.

"The new hoe is very sharp," Macy said. "Aunt Ida was telling me a little about Mr. Toyama. What was he like?"

"Toyama was a pleasant enough fellow. A hard worker." Uncle Emory looked as if thinking back, smiling a little. "He did a lot of fishing and sold most of his catch in town."

"Uncle Emory enjoyed fishing with him from time to time," Aunt Ida said, her expression warm with memory. She rested the teapot on its stand to listen to her husband with a fond smile.

"There was this one time," Uncle Emory said, as crinkles appeared at the corners of his eyes. "The two of us were fishing in his old rowboat, and he hooked a big one. We never did see that fish. It happened so fast."

"What happened?"

"That big fish grabbed his line and jerked Toyama head over boots right off the end of the boat and into the bay."

Macy nearly dropped her fork. "Did he drown?"

"Uncle Emory would never have let that happen," Aunt Ida assured her.

"For a while there, I thought he might be a goner," Uncle Emory said. "Then here comes his hand out of the water, grabbing for the boat. I hauled him in and I'll be darned if he didn't come up laughing."

"Laughing!" Macy thought she must have heard wrong.

"Laughing," Uncle Emory assured her. "Toyama said he thought the fish must have been the ghost of his cranky old neighbor. The woman always had it in for him when she was living."

Macy chuckled with them, though she wasn't sure the story was funny. And now Mr. Toyama was in an internment camp and Uncle Emory was using his tools. She pushed unsettling questions aside. This was as good a time as any to ask about borrowing the wheelbarrow to collect scrap metal.

"It won't be any help to you," Uncle Emory answered, turning to his radio. "The wheelbarrow needs a new tire, and we won't be getting one while rubber is rationed."

"We've already talked about that old wicker baby buggy in the shed out back," Aunt Ida reminded her.

Uncle Emory nodded. "Good idea, Ida. She won't have trouble with the boys trying to steal her tin cans. None of them is likely to run off with a baby buggy!"

Macy giggled. Maybe the buggy would be better

than the wheelbarrow. Even Christopher Adams wouldn't risk being teased by grabbing a baby buggy full of scrap and pushing it through town.

On Sunday, Macy came downstairs wondering if anyone knew it was her birthday, her twelfth. That was important, but maybe not to the Farrells. Rain and wind had battered the coast for most of the week. After church, the sun broke through like a special birthday welcome.

Aunt Ida handed her a card from Papa. "This came for you yesterday, but your papa would want you to have it today for your actual birthday."

Macy tried to swallow her disappointment that Papa hadn't come in person. A note in the card wished her a happy day and said that he was sorry not to be there. With gas rationed and tires impossible to replace, he had to limit his driving.

Uncle Emory surprised her by suggesting a birthday walk on the beach.

"I know you've wanted to go to the beach, but it's too dangerous on your own. You might not see a sub surfacing out there in the waves until the Japs were already on the beach with their rifles."

"I'll keep watching the water," she promised.

He patted the binoculars he wore at his belt. "I'll watch the water. This looks like a good day for you and Aunt Ida to take a look along the wave slope. A storm like this last one may have brought any number of treasures."

One of his rare smiles warmed his face. "Maybe the sea washed in something just in time for your birthday, a pretty rock or shell you can put on your windowsill for a souvenir."

Aunt Ida's smile made her look younger and a little bit mischievous. "They say gold pieces from a wrecked Spanish ship sometimes wash ashore at Cannon Beach up north. I don't see any reason the waves couldn't wash one of them down here."

Treasure! And sand and ocean. Macy could hardly wait. She all but skipped ahead of the Farrells as they walked up the gravel road toward the highway. The salty, mysterious scent of the ocean was already stronger, along with the restless rush of waves.

Before they crossed the highway, Aunt Ida reached for her hand. "Cars cut a pretty pace on the paved road. You wouldn't believe how fast some of them drive through here, even with the speed limit lowered to thirty-five miles per hour during the war."

Macy clasped the hand Aunt Ida held out to her, but inside she was still skipping. At last, she would walk on the beach. It had been so near all the time she'd been here. At night, she leaned out her window just to listen to waves rolling onto the sand.

"Now, I need your promise," Uncle Emory warned. "You're to stay close by, and if we see anything suspicious, you run for the highway and home the moment we tell you."

"Suspicious? Like what?"

"Like that submarine I was talking about earlier."

"Good heavens, Em, you'll have the girl begging to go back to the valley. Let her enjoy a day on the beach."

"Enjoy your day," he told Macy seriously, "but stay near enough that we can keep you safe."

Macy promised, wondering who was right: Aunt Ida, who didn't seem worried, or Uncle Emory, who expected to see the enemy behind every wave.

As far as she could tell, the waves were just waves. After crossing the highway and railroad tracks to follow a trail between the humps of a sand dune, she gave all her attention to the beach, which seemed to stretch forever in both directions.

She'd wanted to come here for so long. If an enemy stormed the beach today and ruined everything, she was going to be really mad.

The wave slope, where the tide stopped coming in and began going out, held heaps of driftwood, shells, and seaweed, all arranged and left behind like a giant scalloped tablecloth. Macy couldn't wait to explore.

"Don't go too far," Aunt Ida warned. "I'll find a nice log to shelter behind. The wind's coming up strong."

Mr. Farrell—Uncle Emory, Macy reminded herself again—was already scanning the waves for submarines. While Aunt Ida settled behind a large driftwood log out of the wind, Macy ran to see what the storm had washed in.

Seagulls shrieked overhead while she collected pieces of oddly shaped driftwood. One looked like a fish, another like a long-legged bird. A third might have been a submarine. She decided not to keep that one.

Below the driftwood and seaweed, rocks tumbled in the waves. Some of them glowed as if with an inner light. Agates! She ran to collect one before the next wave washed it out. It was an amber color.

She held it to the sunlight to look into the translucent depths. Maybe she would leave all the driftwood, but she was keeping this.

Uncle Emory stood on a nearby dune with his binoculars. As Macy started toward him with the agate, she noticed a glint of reflected light from under some driftwood on the wave slope. Curious, she walked closer.

CHAPTER 29

A perfect globe of heavy translucent blue-tinted glass lay almost covered in driftwood and seaweed. Macy picked it out, tossing aside a long hollow length of kelp. It was hard to believe that this beautiful float had traveled all the way across the ocean after holding up a fishing net somewhere far away, maybe even Japan.

"Drop it!" Uncle Emory's shout rang from the dune. He skidded down the steep bank, spraying sand to either side before landing near Macy. "Drop that thing before it explodes in your hands."

"It's just a glass float."

"You can't see into that thing, not clearly. There could be a bomb inside just waiting to bump

up against one of our ships and blow it sky-high."
He snatched it from her and hurled it onto a bank
of jagged rocks holding tide pools at the waterline.

Macy gasped. "Don't!"

She was too late. Shattered glass flew. Macy
couldn't help thinking of Miss Tokyo. The doll
wasn't made of glass, but she could be damaged.
Uncle Emory could destroy her like the float.

If the float had held a bomb, they'd have both
been dangerously close. But there were only heavy
shards of glass on the wet sand and rock.

Uncle Emory looked pleased. "That's that. Did
you have something to show me?"

He admired the agate, but Macy's pleasure
in the stone had faded. Uncle Emory worried too
much. There hadn't been a bomb in the float.
Maybe there weren't any submarines in the water.
Uncle Emory and Aunt Ida should allow her to play
on the beach every nice day.

There was no point asking to come to the beach
alone. She kicked her way toward Aunt Ida through
the silvered driftwood and glossy green kelp along
the wave slope.

Another mass of long bladelike leaves curled
just ahead. Macy put all her frustration into kicking

the mass apart. Her foot hit something that rolled. Rosy glass glinted beneath the green lengths.

Another float? Macy glanced toward the dune, where Uncle Emory was scanning the waves again. Quickly, she knelt and pushed the seaweed clear. The float was a perfect heavy globe of rose-tinted glass. She lifted it to peer into the center.

No bomb inside. Of course not. It was just a float, washed free of a fisherman's net, but what a pretty one. She had to save it. But how could she? Uncle Emory would smash it as quickly as he'd smashed the more common blue float.

She grabbed a nearby length of driftwood and used it to poke innocently at the sand with one hand while snuggling the rosy float close to her body on the side away from Uncle Emory. Logs had washed down from somewhere and been storm-tossed and sun-bleached on the higher part of the beach.

Macy walked to wave-piled drift near the first rise of the dunes. Kneeling on the far side of the biggest log, she dug a nest of soft sand.

Miss Tokyo would love to see the rosy color, she told herself as she arranged driftwood over the glass, hiding it. Satisfied that no one would see it, she sat back on her heels. How could she keep the float safe or even come back for it when she wasn't allowed to come to the beach alone?

That night as she lay pressed to the space between the wall and the bed, she told Miss Tokyo about the shattered float and the hidden one. "We have to keep you secret, so don't make a sound!"

That made her giggle, because of course she made all the sounds for Miss Tokyo. Why was she warning the doll to keep quiet?

And yet, when she didn't talk for the doll, she could feel words pressing inside her that Miss Tokyo would say if she could talk.

"Did I tell you about the scrap collection? I haven't had time to gather Mr. Oakes's cans, but luckily his nephew hasn't come yet."

"Maybe he won't come, Macy-chan," she made the doll answer, knowing the hope was her own.

"I only had the cans Aunt Ida gave me when we turned them in after school on Friday. The other girls had more, but when I added mine, we were ahead of the boys, so everyone was happy."

"They'll be happier when you take in Mr. Oakes's cans," the doll answered in her high voice.

Macy grinned, thinking Miss Tokyo was right

and looking forward to next Saturday, when she would take in the baby buggy filled with tin cans and surprise them all.

The week passed quickly. Macy had hoped to run back to the dune for the float on her way home from school, but Linda from her class lived farther down the highway and walked with her each day.

There was no reason to keep the float a secret from Linda, except that Linda might go after it herself. *It's mine,* Macy told herself silently, *and it's in danger.*

During breakfast on Saturday morning, static blared from the shortwave radio as usual while Uncle Emory twisted the dials. Suddenly, a woman's voice came through, startling them all.

"Listen!" Uncle Emory exclaimed as an announcer identified the station. "I've tuned in Japan!"

"So, Soldier Joe," the young woman said in accented English through a blur of static, "do you remember dolls from America? Maybe your big sisters saved money to buy one. Maybe your mother made clothes for a doll. This was fifteen years ago, Joe. You and your fellow soldiers were little boys then. Do you remember?"

In a low voice, Macy said, "She's talking about Friendship Dolls."

"Your sisters wrote sweet letters, Joe," the woman said as the static faded. "The letters asked little girls in Japan to be kind to the dolls and love them."

Aunt Ida said, "She's aiming her talk at our soldiers, isn't she, the way that awful Tokyo Rose does with her broadcasts? Why is she talking about dolls?"

"All the way from Japan and coming in clear as can be." Uncle Emory beamed at his radio as if he'd built it from scratch and it was suddenly performing properly. Macy leaned closer to hear the Japanese woman's broadcast.

"Do you wonder what happened to those sweet dollies, Joe? We gave them parties when they came. It's sad, though, Joe. Our great General Tōjō says they're symbols of the enemy. So sad. No more parties."

Macy felt her eyes getting wide. All those dolls — more than twelve thousand of them — were seen as enemies in Japan, just the way Miss Tokyo was seen as an enemy in Stanby.

"Our soldiers treated the dolls the way they will treat you, Joe," the woman's voice continued through new static. "They smashed their heads with rifle butts. Bam! Bam! Bam! And our little children? They watched and clapped their hands."

"No," Macy exclaimed. "Oh, no!"

"My land," Aunt Ida said with a gasp.

"I don't believe they clapped," Macy said. "They're just children. They wouldn't clap when dolls were smashed. They wouldn't!"

"Our countries are at war," Uncle Emory said, as if Macy might have forgotten even for a minute. "You've got to expect things like that."

Aunt Ida said, "The Japanese sent some dolls to children here in return." Then her mouth clamped tight, as if she'd just remembered that Macy was here because she cared too much for one of those big Japanese dolls.

"I'd like to put a bullet through any doll they sent," Uncle Emory said. "We don't want their trash here any more than they want dolls from us."

Macy saw him catch an anxious look from Aunt Ida. When he turned to Macy, he looked the way the pastor at home looked when he was about to make an important point. "Pearl Harbor brought our country together against the enemy. We won't stand for anybody attacking us."

He waited as if he expected an answer. Macy could only think of little children watching soldiers smash the American dolls. She would never believe that those children had clapped their hands.

Uncle Emory's voice roughened. "That's why you're collecting scrap. Just don't forget the Victory Garden. Every bit of food we grow for ourselves means food we don't have to buy. And that leaves more canned goods available for our soldiers."

"And more ration coupons saved," Aunt Ida added.

Macy nodded and pushed away her bowl.

Aunt Ida said, "Before you start on the Victory Garden, dear, will you help me take the sheets off the beds so I can get them in the wash?"

Fresh horror swept through Macy. Aunt Ida was going to take the sheets off the beds. She might pull the beds away from the wall. She would see Miss Tokyo. And then she would tell Uncle Emory, and he would destroy the Japanese doll.

"I'll bring my sheets downstairs," she said quickly.

"You do that, dear. I want to sweep behind and under the beds, and it's easier when the coverings are off."

The rice puffs Macy had eaten felt like they were exploding all over again inside her stomach.

She gulped down a last spoonful because the Farrells didn't approve of waste, and pushed to her feet. "I'll get my sheets right now. I . . . I want to get started collecting cans as soon as I can."

She raced up the stairs without waiting for an answer. She had to get Miss Tokyo away. Where could she hide the doll? It didn't matter. She would find a place. First she had to get Miss Tokyo out of the house.

She pictured the doll standing against a target, maybe with a blindfold over her eyes, while Uncle Emory aimed his rifle.

By the time she reached the top of the stairs, she was gasping for breath. She grabbed the door frame, swung around it, and paused, trying to hear over the pounding in her ears.

Downstairs, Aunt Ida hummed as she walked into the big bedroom on the first floor.

Macy rushed to her bed, dropped to her knees, and squirmed beneath. She grabbed Miss Tokyo and backed out, pulling the doll with her. "I'm sorry," she whispered. "We have to get you away. Right now."

The blanket had fallen from the doll's face. Macy paused to look at her, seeing as if for the first time the doll's gentle eyes and sweet hint of a smile. "Mama," she whispered into the air, "you don't think the children clapped. Do you?"

She couldn't hear Mama answer or even answer for her in the high voice they always gave the doll. Why wasn't Mama answering?

Maybe Mama didn't think Macy could get Miss Tokyo to safety. "I promised," she said. "I promised Mama and Hap. I'll save you, Miss Tokyo. I promised to save you for them."

She heard tears in the voice she gave the doll as she answered shakily, "Will you save me for yourself, too, Macy-chan?"

A tear slipped from Macy's cheek onto the doll's face. She brushed it away with one hand. "Yes. I love you, and now you have to hide again, but not under the bed." Carefully, she rewrapped the blanket around the doll, then pulled sheets from the bed and crumpled them around the bundle.

Where would the doll be safe? The garage? The Farrells took firewood from the stack every day, but the stack lined one entire wall. There must have been at least a hundred pieces piled there. Maybe Miss Tokyo could hide under the far end.

She carried the blanket-wrapped doll to the stairway and listened with her entire body. A fresh burst of static told her that Uncle Emory was still working with his radio. She didn't hear Aunt Ida, but time was running out. She could feel minutes rushing past.

Quietly, she moved down the stairs. Her chest hurt as she held her breath, trying so hard to hear that she wouldn't let her own breathing make a sound.

She was almost to the bottom of the stairs when she heard Aunt Ida humming, the sound coming closer. Macy didn't have to see her to know that Aunt Ida was heading for the stairs with her broom and dustpan.

CHAPTER 30

If you can't go back, go ahead as if you mean it, Macy told herself, repeating one of Mama's favorite sayings.

She put a smile on her face and started down the stairs, passing Mrs. Farrell. "Bye, Aunt Ida. I'm off to do my part for the war."

"Leave your sheets at the bottom of the stairs," Aunt Ida said. She looked more closely at Macy's bundle before adding, "Do you want your blanket washed, too, dear?"

The blanket poked out between the sheets. Macy hesitated, thinking fast. "No. I promised Mr.

Oakes I'd pick up his empty tin cans. And I . . . uh . . . need it."

"Of course you do. You'll want to cover the empty cans so they won't blow off," the woman said, her expression clearing. "That's thinking ahead, dear. Good for you."

Relief swept through Macy. "Thank you, Aunt Ida. I have to hurry now."

She ran down the rest of the stairs, clutching Miss Tokyo in her bundled blanket as she left the sheets, fearing at every step to be called back.

Inside the open garage, she swept her glance around and discovered a folded brown canvas tarp. It was nearly the color of the firewood. She lowered her bundle to the garage floor, whipped open the tarp, and quickly rolled Miss Tokyo from the blanket onto the tarp, taking care to fold the heavy cloth over the doll's head and feet.

"They'll take in firewood from nearest the door," Macy whispered, and moved down the garage to the end of the woodpile. She lifted several pieces of wood near the end, hoisted Miss Tokyo and the tarp into the hollow she'd made, and carefully placed lengths of wood on top.

She stepped back to pick up the blanket and check her work. Anyone looking closely would see the tarp and wonder why it was in there, but people pretty much saw what they expected to see, and the Farrells expected to see a neat stack of firewood.

Miss Tokyo was safe. For a while.

"I'm sorry," Macy told her softly. "It can't be pleasant in there, but it's the best I can do for now, Miss T."

In her head, the doll's high voice answered, "Do not worry, Macy-chan. I know you will come for me."

"Soon," Macy promised. "Soon, I hope. Now I need to get Mr. Oakes's tin cans."

Mr. Oakes came outside to help load his big pile of empty cans into the baby buggy. They worked together to fasten the blanket over the cans to keep the wind from blowing them away. Macy thanked him for letting her take them and silently thanked him again for turning her near-lie to Aunt Ida into a truth.

"When do you expect your great-nephew?" she asked as they loaded the buggy.

Mr. Oakes settled his striped knit cap lower over his ears as if the cold bothered him. The little bells on top jingled, making Macy smile despite herself. "Pretty soon, I should think," he answered.

"Cee-Cee's mother says folk here have contacted her, worried about my light spilling out at night."

Who had contacted the nephew's mother? Macy wondered. The Farrells? Didn't they know she ran out each evening to check Mr. Oakes's curtains and warn him if light showed? Maybe they did know and meant to spare her.

Mr. Oakes turned his grimace into a smile, as if determined to make the best of a difficult situation. "Cee-Cee will be good company. For you, too, I expect. You must be about the same age."

"He'll be in my class, then. And looking for tin cans." She couldn't help glancing at her loaded baby buggy. "Maybe I should leave some for him."

"No, Miss Macy, you take those along. He can wait. I'll be opening twice as many once he gets here with his growing boy's appetite."

Macy wanted to say that the boy named Cee-Cee would expect more than canned soup, but she didn't dare offer Aunt Ida's homemade bread without asking first. "I'd better go, then," she said instead, adding quickly, "Thank you."

As she pushed the buggy over the rough gravel to the highway and alongside it toward town, she wondered about Cee-Cee. *I hope he's nice. He's sure to be nicer than Christopher Adams.*

But that wasn't fair. In his own way, Christopher had been nice. Sometimes. Rarely, but sometimes. Why was she even thinking of him? He probably wasn't thinking of her at all.

When her nightly check showed light slanting from Mr. Oakes's window again, Macy ran through a light rain and knocked on the door. He opened it, and she pointed past him to a stack of books on the windowsill holding the curtain off-kilter.

Mr. Oakes shook his head. "I get distracted and set them down wherever I happen to be. Many thanks for noticing, Miss Macy."

When he walked over to the window to straighten the curtain, Macy leaned curiously into the room. "You sure have a lot of books."

"My great pleasure and biggest fault," he said, smiling. "I often catch the Greyhound bus up on the highway and ride to our county seat at Tillamook to browse through bookstores."

He turned to a table and picked up a book with a glossy cover. "I found this one for you. You mentioned enjoying your mother's book of pictures from Japan. Maybe you'll like this."

He held out the book with a cloud of cherry blossoms on the cover. Macy felt her mouth shape a silent *Oh.* Inside, picture after picture showed shrines, temples, and masses of blossoming trees. "Thank you." She clasped the book close. "I can almost feel Mama looking through it with me."

"It's my thanks to you," he said, "for keeping an eye on my blackout problem."

She looked through the book again, but clapped it shut with a sudden awful thought. "I won't be able to keep it. The Farrells hate Japanese things."

"Keep the book here, then," he said. "My porch is usually sheltered from the rain. You're welcome to sit out there and look through your book any time you like."

She felt as if a blackout curtain couldn't dim her smile as she thanked him again and handed the book back for safekeeping. Happiness stayed with her all the way home to her chores.

The Farrells had agreed to set a daily time limit to clearing the garden and rolling bandages. Once her work was finished, Macy was free to do as she wished until supper and homework. Of course, she was not to venture near the beach by herself, since the enemy might invade at any time, according to Uncle Emory.

Aunt Ida hesitated when Macy explained that Mr. Oakes had invited her to read books from his collection, but as long as Macy promised to remain on the porch, she agreed. Uncle Emory said he was relieved to learn that the many trips Mr. Oakes made on the Greyhound bus were to explore bookstores and not to meet with a group of spies, as some people feared.

Macy almost smiled at that, thinking what Papa might say about Uncle Emory's fears. Still, she heard the war reports on the shortwave radio. The war was terrible. Maybe she should take those fears seriously.

What would Hap think of her enjoying pictures of beautiful places in Japan? The question came suddenly. Hap had died because of enemy soldiers from the land of beautiful shrines and blossoming trees.

"Angry people make the most noise," she said softly. "Nobody hears from the gentle people who live there, too, people like the doll maker who made Miss Tokyo. Hap loved Miss Tokyo. He would understand."

Her corner on Mr. Oakes's porch was comfortably out of the rain so often streaming from the eaves. She nestled in a big rattan chair on a cushion Mr. Oakes kept dry in his cabin until she came for it. While she listened to the rain, she imagined herself walking through a tunnel of blossoming cherry trees. She was careful not to imagine falling bombs or the sound of rifles among those trees. She carried her journal in her pocket and wrote short notes from her cozy corner.

The Farrells' woodpile grew smaller near the back door. The potbelly stove in the front room took a steady supply, but there was still a safe amount between the kitchen and Miss Tokyo.

"Macy," Aunt Ida said after only a week of afternoon free time spent on Mr. Oakes's front porch, "it's too wet to work in the garden, but before you leave today, please bring in an armload of firewood."

"Right away, Aunt Ida." Macy pulled on her coat and started for the garage.

Aunt Ida called after her, "Take wood from the far end this time, dear. Uncle Emory will be ordering another load next week. We may as well begin clearing space for it at the back."

Macy was glad she was turned away so Aunt Ida wouldn't see the shock on her face. Miss Tokyo had to be moved. She had to be moved now.

CHAPTER 31

In the garage, Macy pulled the firewood from on top of Miss Tokyo. She carried the wood into the house, then hurried back. Her stomach clenched with fear that Uncle Emory would come into the garage and find the doll wrapped in the tarp.

What to do with her? She stood by the woodpile and glanced around. Many people kept spaces like this crowded with castoffs of all kinds, but Aunt Ida wasn't the sort to keep everything. There was nowhere to leave the doll where she wouldn't be noticed at once.

The rattan buggy might be the answer. No one would wonder why she was pushing it away from the house. They were used to seeing her with it.

Quickly, Macy pulled the buggy from the corner where she'd left it. She settled Miss Tokyo inside, but now what? Could she cover the doll with cans and say she was waiting for enough to fill the buggy before turning them in? Did Mr. Oakes have enough for that?

As she pushed the buggy across the road, she knew in her heart that this plan wasn't going to work. She couldn't think of anything else to do.

The buggy bumped over rough weeds and rocks to the back where her neighbor tossed his empty cans. There weren't very many.

Macy considered the small cabin held above the ground by a wood foundation with spaces between the supports. Could she push the doll beneath the cabin? Would rats chew Miss Tokyo's kimono?

Shivering, Macy rubbed tears from her face, tears she hadn't been aware of crying.

From the open doorway, Mr. Oakes called out to her. "Child, what is it?"

She looked at him, feeling like a deer caught in headlights. There was nothing left but the truth. "Mr. Farrell" — she couldn't think of him as Uncle Emory — "wants to kill my doll, and I don't have anywhere to hide her."

"Kill your doll! Why?" Mr. Oakes came down

the back stairs and over to the buggy. He looked in surprise at the tarp. "You've hidden your doll in there?"

"She's not exactly my doll." Macy's voice broke on the confession. "She's from Japan. She has a kimono and everything."

Her mind and heart flooded with the thought of Mr. Farrell shooting a bullet into the doll's head. Her knees wouldn't hold her, and she slipped to the grass with one hand on the buggy. "He'll kill her. I know he will. I can't let him do that."

"May I see her?"

With unsteady hands, Macy unrolled the heavy canvas from Miss Tokyo. Part of her was relieved to see that the tarp hadn't messed up the doll and her pretty kimono. The rest of her filled with dread.

Mr. Oakes whistled softly. "Was she your mother's?"

"Not exactly." Macy drew a deep breath she felt all the way to her toes. "Mama loved her, but she belongs to the museum where my papa is the curator."

"A museum. I begin to understand."

"The people in town said she was a symbol of the enemy. They were going to burn her in a bonfire."

"Ahh. And you've spirited her away to save her."

"Nobody knows I have her, but if Mr. Farrell finds out, he'll shoot her. He said so. He said the big Friendship Dolls the Japanese children sent to America a long time ago should all be shot!"

Mr. Oakes nodded. "Mr. Farrell has a lot of patriotic spirit. A little more than necessary, maybe."

Macy thought there was no *maybe* about it. "He shot some fishing floats because they came from Japan. And he broke one I found on the beach."

"Well." Mr. Oakes settled his cap a little more warmly over his ears. "Our concern is what we are to do with the doll."

Macy looked into Miss Tokyo's gentle eyes. "I won't let him shoot her."

"No, no, that can't be allowed." Mr. Oakes considered for a long moment. "I'll tell you what, Miss Macy. I have a closet off the kitchen that's scarcely used. It might not be pleasant for her, but your doll could wait there for the duration."

Macy gasped for a breath that felt a long time coming. "Oh, thank you. Thank you so much!"

"You're very welcome." He reached into the buggy for the doll. "Does this beautiful young lady have a name?"

"Miss Tokyo. The dolls the children sent all have names that say where they came from." Would that change his mind? Was the name too much a reminder of the people fighting American soldiers? Killing them? She'd heard Uncle Emory's radio news, and it was horrible. War was horrible.

But Mr. Oakes didn't seem troubled by the name. "We'd better get Miss Tokyo out of sight. You come on up to the door and watch where I put her so you'll know where she's waiting for you."

Relief lightened Macy's steps as she followed Mr. Oakes and the doll to the back door. Still, as she watched through the kitchen while her neighbor opened a narrow closet and placed the doll inside, she half-expected Mr. Farrell to show up with his gun.

Uncle Emory, she told herself. *I have to call him that or he'll want to know why I stopped. I might forget and mention Miss T.*

All the next week after school and chores, Macy nestled into the wicker chair on Mr. Oakes's porch and looked through the book he had given her. Softly, she spoke with the doll hiding nearby. "Here's a picture of fishing cormorants, Miss Tokyo. Like the ones in Mama's book. Do you remember?"

The high voice she gave the doll wavered in a reply. "*Hai.* Yes, Macy-chan, I remember."

"I remember, too," Macy whispered. "I will never forget."

Hap would understand, even though the horrible war makers in Miss Tokyo's country had killed him.

The Farrells weren't able to roast a turkey for Thanksgiving dinner, but Aunt Ida lifted a beautifully browned roast chicken from the oven while Macy mashed potatoes. Uncle Emory hummed a church hymn as he tuned his big shortwave radio.

When they all sat down at the table, Uncle Emory said a blessing, including thanks that turkeys were going to our boys overseas. Aunt Ida suggested they each say what they were thankful for today. Smiling at Macy, she said, "I'm thankful to have Macy join our family. She brings fresh energy into our lives and reminds us to look with wonder at natural things like the ocean and sand and even seagulls."

Macy wanted to say something nice back, but she wasn't happy to be there. She missed Papa and Lily and even Christopher Adams. As she hesitated, Uncle Emory said, "Well, I'm thankful we've finally turned the corner on the war. Our boys won a great battle in North Africa. They've got a handle on it now. The first thing we know, the war will be over and they'll be home again, telling us all about it."

Macy wished she could say she was happy to have a letter from Nick, but she hadn't received one since moving here. Aunt Ida said it probably took the post office time to figure out where she was.

"Macy, dear?" Aunt Ida prompted.

Macy looked from one to the other. "I'm happy that you are kind to me."

"As if we could be anything else!" Aunt Ida's eyes got shiny. Macy hoped that didn't mean tears, even if they were happy ones. But Aunt Ida motioned to Uncle Emory. "Are you going to slice the turkey, dear? It's not there for decoration, you know."

"Turkey!"

"We're pretending," Macy explained.

Aunt Ida said quickly, "I expect the Pilgrims would have served a chicken if they couldn't find a turkey in time."

Macy giggled. "Maybe they did serve chicken, and the history books made it look bigger."

"Pretending," Uncle Emory said. "In my mind, that's dangerously close to a lie. And lies hurt in the end." He gave Aunt Ida a meaningful look.

What did that look mean? Macy rushed to Aunt Ida's defense. "I'm thankful we can pretend our chicken is a turkey. It looks yummy, Aunt Ida, and smells even yummier!"

Aunt Ida smiled and patted Macy's hand, but the laughter had gone from her eyes.

On Saturday, a strange car parked outside Mr. Oakes's cabin. Macy balanced the hot flatiron on its plate beside the handkerchiefs she was ironing for Aunt Ida and watched through the window. A woman stepped from the driver's side of the car. A boy climbed from the backseat, bending over and pulling a suitcase with him.

She said aloud, "Cee-Cee's here."

Aunt Ida lifted a tray of cookies from the oven. "He's just in time to try my honey cookies."

"The ones that save sugar for the army cooks," Macy said, remembering.

"That's right. Uncle Em's favorites. Mr. Oakes's great-nephew is sure to like them. Every little boy likes cookies." She smiled at Macy. "Every big boy, too. Why don't you take a batch over? It will give you a chance to get acquainted."

The boy's mother drove away before the cookies had cooled enough to be put onto a plate. "She's not very nice," Macy said. "She brought him here and left."

That caused a shocked look from Aunt Ida, but Macy was remembering the way Papa had left so soon after bringing her here. That boy across the street must be feeling abandoned, the way she had then. Maybe the cookies would help.

She arranged them carefully and carried them across the street.

As soon as she knocked, the door to Mr. Oakes's cabin swung open. The new boy looked out, his eyes going wide, but he caught the plate of cookies as it nearly fell from Macy's hands. "You're the nice girl across the street?" In his voice, she heard, *How could my uncle make that mistake?*

In almost the same moment, she exclaimed in horror, "You're Cee-Cee?"

"Chris," he corrected sharply. "Nobody but my uncle calls me by that baby name."

"Your uncle, and maybe me." She liked feeling a sense of power as she looked Christopher Adams straight in the eyes. "Cee-Cee. That's kind of cute."

"I'll say this once. When I was a kid, I couldn't say Christopher. It sounded like Cee-Cee, and for a while that's what they called me. Now I'm just Chris. Got that?"

She was tempted to grab back the plate of cookies, but she wasn't forgetting how it felt to be left somewhere you didn't want to be. "Truce. I'll call you 'Just Chris' like everybody else. Enjoy the cookies, Just Chris."

He scowled. "Don't make me throw sand down your neck."

"You'll have to catch me first."

"You think I can't?"

"That's right, Cee-Cee." Turning, she raced for home. When she glanced over her shoulder, she saw Chris grabbing sand from the bucket on his uncle's front porch.

He was faster than she expected. She saw him cut across the Farrells' big front yard to head her off. She veered toward the open garage and had just reached the steps to the back door when he caught up.

He grabbed her collar.

She shrieked.

The door flew open. "What in the world?" Aunt Ida exclaimed.

Chris's hand fell away, but not before a few

grains of sand had trickled down the back of Macy's neck. She shook her collar to get rid of them. "Aunt Ida, this is Christopher Adams, Mr. Oakes's great-nephew. He was in my class in Stanby."

"Imagine that!" Aunt Ida said, smiling. "How nice that you're already friends."

Chris looked at Macy with an expression that said Aunt Ida was as mixed up as his great-uncle.

"We're not friends," Macy corrected. "We don't even like each other."

"You don't?" Aunt Ida looked from one to the other. "Why not?"

"When you opened the door," Macy exclaimed with a rush of indignation, "he was trying to put sand down my collar."

Aunt Ida's face relaxed. "Oh, well, you are friends, then. You just don't know it yet. Come in, Christopher. Do you like hot cocoa?"

Macy shook her head violently.

Chris grinned. "Sure, cocoa would be great." He winced as Macy pinched his arm. "But then I have to get back to Uncle Del."

Aunt Ida went into the house, leaving the door open. Chris turned to Macy, his blue eyes more intense than she had ever seen them. "We can be friends. If we try hard enough."

Was he kidding? She stared after him in astonishment as he followed Aunt Ida into the kitchen. Having Christopher Adams living across the street might be even more difficult than she'd thought. *What was she going to do about Miss Tokyo?*

CHAPTER 32

While they sipped hot cocoa and ate honey cookies, Aunt Ida asked Chris about school and sports — all the boring questions grown-ups always asked.

Macy was glad of it. Everything felt normal. She could pretend she wasn't terrified inside. All the time she had waited for Mr. Oakes's great-nephew to arrive, she had thought he would be like Mr. Oakes. She'd hoped he would help protect Miss Tokyo.

But the nephew was Christopher Adams. He'd been kind the awful day of the bonfire. He'd even carried Miss Tokyo to the museum for her. And a little while ago, he'd sort of said they could be friends. But what would he say if he learned she'd brought the doll here and that Miss Tokyo was hiding in his great-uncle's closet?

Uncle Emory had said he'd like to shoot all the Japanese dolls. If Christopher told him about Miss Tokyo, Uncle Emory would head straight for his gun. A shiver ran through Macy. She swallowed a gulp of hot cocoa, but it couldn't warm the chill she felt inside.

"Has Macy told you about her scrap collecting?" Aunt Ida asked Chris. "She has everyone in school competing to bring in the most tin. And every bit of fat from the kitchen goes to the war effort. She watches our ration coupons, too, making sure they cover everything we need. No black-market goods will come into this house."

Chris glanced at Macy, who felt her face getting warm. To Aunt Ida he said, "I'm glad to hear she's turned into a super-patriot. I suppose that's because Nick —"

Aunt Ida cut him off. "Of course she's proud of all our fighting men. Would you like to take some cookies to your uncle, dear?"

"He already has some," Macy reminded her, wondering why Aunt Ida had cut in like that when she'd been trying to draw Chris out. "I nearly dropped the plate when Chris answered the door."

"And you'll be in the same class at school," Aunt Ida said, as if that were the best news ever. "You can walk together."

"Uh, well, I can show you where it is," Macy told Chris. If he agreed to walk with her, that would be his choice, not Aunt Ida's.

"Sure," he said, getting to his feet. "I'd better get back to Uncle Del now. Meet you at the road Monday morning?"

"Okay." Inside, she felt her nerves tightening. His uncle Del must have been keeping the doll out of sight in that closet. Maybe some heavy clothes hung in front of her.

She was going to stay away. She'd have to be careful what she said every minute she spent with Christopher Adams. She couldn't let him find out about Miss Tokyo.

She lay awake late into the night and the next night, too, picturing Chris looking into his uncle's closet, but he didn't rush across the street dragging the doll behind him so she began to relax a little. On Monday, they left their houses at the same time and walked to school together.

Macy wasn't surprised to see that Chris fit easily

into the new school. *I had to set up scrap collecting,* she thought. *All he has to do is push his hair back and smile.*

Linda turned from the desk ahead to whisper, "He has the bluest eyes ever! You went to the same school? Lucky! Does he have a girlfriend?"

"I don't know! I left ages ago." The words sounded defensive. She added, "There was this girl Rachel. But he hasn't said anything about her."

"Then they must have broken up," Linda said. "You're friends. He'd have told you if he was sad to move away from her."

"We're not friends! We're enemies." Maybe she shouldn't have said that, but it was annoying to watch Linda drooling over Christopher Adams.

"What happened?" Linda's eyes went wide. "Did he try to kiss you?"

"What? No!" Macy felt her face getting hot. Why hadn't the teacher told Linda to stop whispering and turn around? "He broke something that mattered to me. On purpose. That's all."

Macy pulled open her spelling book and stared at squiggles that didn't even look like letters for a moment. Then Miss Ross said, "Linda, turn around and sit straight, please," and Macy could breathe easily again.

Macy was sure Chris would walk home with his new friends after school. But the only one going their way was Linda, so he fell into step with the two of them, and while Linda giggled and flirted, Macy silently fumed.

Linda asked, "Is this your first time to the beach, Chris?"

"I've visited my uncle before." He glanced toward the dunes. "Anyone else want to go see what the waves have washed in?"

Macy thought at once of the rose-colored float. Should she tell them about it? She couldn't take it to the Farrells'. Chris might as well have it. But he'd probably give it to Linda.

It's mine, Macy told herself, *and I'm keeping it.* Aloud she said, "I have to go home. The Farrells think the beach is dangerous while the war is going on. Besides, I have chores."

"See you tomorrow." Linda looked far too eager to say good-bye.

Every day after school, Linda and Chris went over the dunes to spend half an hour or so exploring the beach while Macy walked the rest of the way home alone. Though she tried not to pay attention, she couldn't help but notice him coming home to his uncle's with his hair windblown and his skin reddened from sun and wind.

Linda began an annoying habit of talking about him as if he belonged to her, saying, "I can't wait for school to let out so Chris and I can go to the beach" or "Chris and I found an amazing tide pool yesterday" or "Chris and I are going to race hermit crabs to see whose gets into the tide pool first."

On Friday, Linda stayed after school for cheerleader practice. As Macy walked along the highway toward home with Chris, she asked before she knew she was going to, "Do you like Linda?"

His eyebrows rose in surprise. "She's okay. I don't think she'd have the nerve to stop just about everybody in town from burning a Japanese doll, though."

Macy was startled to hear him bring up the bonfire. "I saved her, but Papa says I was dumb to defy everybody over a doll."

Chris stopped walking to look at her. His eyes weren't accusing. Were they actually approving? "It was dumb," he said, adding, "Dumb but brave."

"That's me." She didn't know whether to feel praised or insulted and decided to feel praised.

After a few more steps toward home, he turned to her again. "Why did you ask? About Linda, I mean."

Because he had praised her in a Chris sort of way, she risked trusting him. "I want to show you something I found on the beach. If it's still there. But Linda can't have it."

"Okay. Where is it? What is it?"

"I'll show you."

Her conscience pinched, but she hadn't actually promised the Farrells she wouldn't go to the beach without them. So she led Chris over the railroad track and the short road through the dunes.

She remembered exactly where she'd left the rosy float, but she took a moment to breathe deeply of the salt air. She needed to watch the waves rising and breaking and rolling to the sand. Something about the unchanging ocean made her feel safe. Even if Uncle Emory did think the waves were full of enemy submarines.

"So where is it?" Chris demanded.

"This way." She led him to the log, hoping the higher night tides hadn't reclaimed her treasure. No, seaweed still lay in a heap where she'd piled it over the driftwood and glass. Dropping to her knees in the grainy sand, she shoved the kelp aside and lifted out the float.

Chris blew a low, appreciative breath. "Keen!"

When he held out his hand, she hesitated, then let him take the baseball-size globe.

Chris held it up. In the lowering sunlight, the rosy glass glowed as if filled with fire. "You found this?"

"Weeks ago."

"Weeks ago! Why leave it here? The tide could take it."

Macy rose to her feet, frustration rushing through her just as it had on the day she found the float. "I can't take it to the Farrells. Mr. Farrell breaks them. He says anything from Japan should be smashed. I can't let him find the . . . uh . . . the float."

She'd nearly said "the doll." She clamped her lips together, but Chris was too busy admiring the heavy glass globe to notice. "You can't leave it here," he said. "It will wash away any night the tide comes up this high."

"I can't keep it with me."

"I'll take it to Uncle Del. He'll let us have it there."

He would. Of course he would. Mr. Oakes would understand. "Maybe he'll put it in a window," Macy said, "where the sun can light it up like that.

But don't let the blackout curtains hang up on it."

"I'll keep an eye on the curtains," Chris promised. "That's what I'm here for."

"I'm glad."

For a moment, their eyes met and held, sharing the secret of the float, sharing the brush of misty salt air, sharing the rush and fall of the waves, and maybe, she thought, sharing the start of friendship.

"I've got to go now," she said with reluctance. "They'll wonder where I am."

"Right." He walked with her across the dune and down the road to their houses. They were almost there when he said, "I don't know about that float, about keeping it in a window, I mean."

Macy looked at him sharply. "Do you want to take it back to the beach?"

"No, but Uncle Del got in trouble over light showing under his curtains. Someone like Mr. Farrell might call him a traitor for putting a Japanese float in his window."

Macy sucked in a breath so sharp it hurt. They would, when Mr. Oakes had only been nice to her. "We need to hide the float."

"I'll take care of it. Don't worry. I just won't put it in a window for anybody to see."

"Where will you put it?"

"I don't know. Under the couch, maybe. That's where I sleep."

"You sleep under the couch?"

"On the couch!" His grin answered hers.

"With the float under there, you might dream of sailing," she said, "and wake up seasick."

"More likely I'll wake up under the covers thinking I've been swallowed by a whale."

Laughter felt good and made her much happier than the jokes deserved.

CHAPTER 33

On Sunday afternoon as Macy finished folding laundry for Aunt Ida, Chris came to the door. When Aunt Ida answered, he spoke with angry precision. "Please ask Macy to come outside. I want to talk to her."

Aunt Ida exchanged a puzzled glance with Macy before asking, "Is something wrong, dear? Your uncle?"

"My uncle is fine, thank you." He sounded too polite. What was going on? He said again, "I need to talk to Macy."

"Would you like to come in?" Aunt Ida began.

Macy said quickly, "Never mind. I'm right here."

As she came toward the door, Chris said, "Bring your coat," and started toward his uncle's cabin.

Macy snatched up her coat and ran after him. "What's the matter? Why are you acting like this? Is it your uncle?"

"My uncle is well. If you don't count being called a spy because his curtains aren't always tight and he makes mysterious bus trips to Tillamook."

"To buy books!"

"Not everybody knows that. You must have heard talk in school. I sure have."

"But everything can be explained."

They had reached his uncle's stairs. As he led her to the porch and opened the door, he said, "People could understand a Japanese fishing float if they saw it in his window. Something pretty, picked up on the beach. A lot of people have one."

"You want me to move the float?"

Without answering, he stalked toward the closet near the kitchen.

Macy knew what was coming even before he threw open the door.

Miss Tokyo stood in the closet. She looked embarrassed, as if caught holding the change from Mr. Oakes's dresser drawer. Macy felt the same way.

Chris's knuckles turned white on the door frame. For a moment, Macy thought he was going to slam the door shut again. "How could he explain this?" he demanded. "A museum piece. From Japan. Hidden in his home."

Macy felt sick. She hadn't thought about the people who already suspected Mr. Oakes when she left the doll with him. She imagined them now and shivered. *I've put my friend in terrible danger when he's been nice to me.*

Tears choked her as she said, "People at home wanted to kill Miss Tokyo. You know about that, Chris. They weren't going to stop trying just because I left. How could I leave her behind to be burned or worse?"

"She was in storage."

"But I promised! I promised Mama and I promised Hap that I'd keep Miss Tokyo safe. I couldn't go off and leave her to be ruined!"

"So you sneaked her along."

Macy looked unhappily at the doll. "Aunt Ida wanted to sweep under the bed where Miss Tokyo was hiding, so I put her in the woodpile. But then I found out more wood was coming and . . ."

"And you thought nobody'd suspect Uncle Del of hiding her. Right?"

"How could they suspect when they didn't know about her? I was scared, Chris, and he offered to help."

"Wrap the doll in your coat and get her out of here."

Macy knelt quickly and spread her coat on the floor, but then she lowered her head to her arms. Despair spread through her. "What can I do with her?"

"You should have left her at the museum."

"But I couldn't. I told you —"

"What I don't get," Chris said, cutting her off, "is why you want to protect her even now. Don't you care that a Jap sub sank your brother's ship?"

Macy felt blood leave her face. Her hands — her whole body — chilled as if she'd stepped into the cold ocean. She wouldn't . . . she couldn't believe him. Nick's ship? No, he was lying.

She swung around to search Chris's face, her hand clenching over the anchor on her necklace. "Why would you say that?"

The truth was in his face. And in her own memory.

Scenes flashed through her head: Aunt Ida cutting Chris off when he started to talk about Nick. Uncle Emory telling Papa the night they arrived that she should be told. Overhearing Papa telling the pastor in Stanby that she had too much on her shoulders already. The missing letters from Nick!

They had all known and kept the awful truth from her. She knew how it felt to stand in the waves while sand was pulled from beneath her feet. She felt like that now, as if everything she believed were being drained away.

"The ship went down months ago," Chris said. "I thought you knew."

"Nobody told me! Why did they let me think Nick was coming home?"

Chris looked sick, but she couldn't feel sorry for him. Everything roared through her. Papa didn't trust her. No one trusted her. There'd been that fight at school. And being removed. And sent here to live with patriotic people.

It was all because of Miss Tokyo. Everything was Miss Tokyo's fault.

She snatched up the Japanese doll so quickly the doll's head smacked the door frame. "I was good to her. I kept her from a bonfire. I talked to her all the time. Now nobody trusts me. Not even Papa! And Nick's been torpedoed! And it's her fault!"

Chris reached toward the doll's head. "You'll break it."

"I want her to hurt. Like I do!"

Ignoring Chris's hand on her arm, Macy stumbled through the cabin and down the front stairs. The doll felt like a ten-pound log. It was no longer a doll to her, and no longer a friend.

When she rushed through the Farrells' front door, Uncle Emory looked up, startled, from his shortwave radio. "What is it? Has something happened?"

"You said you'd shoot a Japanese doll. Here's one. Shoot her." She dumped the doll on the floor by his chair. "Shoot her now!"

Chris came through the doorway. "I thought she knew about Nick," he said, sounding anguished. "How come she didn't know?"

"Oh, dear." Aunt Ida came to Macy and wrapped one arm about her. "Macy, dear, your papa told us you probably had the doll with you. He said hotheaded people would destroy it if it remained in the museum."

Macy felt her mouth come open. "All this time I've been terrified that Uncle Emory would find out about her and shoot her, and you already knew she was here!"

"We couldn't imagine where," Aunt Ida said.

"Doesn't anybody tell the truth around here?" Chris asked. "She didn't know about her brother. She thought the doll was a secret."

"Her papa didn't want her upset." Aunt Ida stroked Macy's hair. "All we know for certain is that Nick's ship went down. It's possible there were lifeboats. Your papa was waiting for good news before he had to tell you the bad."

Uncle Emory clasped one of Macy's hands to rub warmth back into her skin. "You're thinking with your heart instead of your head, honey. I know because I do the same thing. I did that when I said the dolls should be shot."

"She's the enemy." Macy pointed to the doll.

"That's what I said about my friend. Your loyalty to the doll made me think again. Yoshio Toyama and I had good times together. He had nothing to do with the war. He's a peaceful man. You've made me remember that."

"But he's Japanese."

"Give this a week, honey. Let your mind catch up with your grief. When I said Japanese dolls should be shot, I was angry about the war. I still am, but the doll's not to blame, any more than my friend Yoshio. This doll is important to you. Deep inside, you know that."

Macy clamped her mouth shut on sobs she was determined to keep down. Even to her own ears, she was sounding like Mr. Ames and the others. Maybe they had been right all along.

Chris said, "Macy, if I'd known . . ."

"Don't you apologize. You're the only one who told me the truth. Everybody else lied."

Aunt Ida told Chris quietly, "Leave her to us, dear. She'll get through this. She has a strong spirit."

"Go," Macy told him. When he left, glancing back, she called after him in silence, *Stay*.

"Strong and sensible," Uncle Emory said. "Macy, when the government men took Yoshio Toyama away, I said, 'Great! Get that Jap fellow out of here.' It took you to bring back memories, to remind me of the good man he is."

Macy heard what he was saying, that Mr. Toyama had nothing to do with the war but was blamed because he was Japanese. Like Betsy Oshima and her family at home.

Like Miss Tokyo.

But the Japanese had torpedoed Nick. And killed

Hap. A battle raged inside her. She wanted to listen to reason, but she kept picturing Nick's ship, like one they showed in the movie theaters just as a torpedo hit.

"You should burn those tools marked with Japanese writing," she said, reluctant to let go of the fury that had driven her across the street with the doll.

"No, I'm not going to burn them," Uncle Emory said. "Your anger with the doll is like a mirror to the way I've been seeing the world around me and just as narrow-sighted. I'm going to take special care of those tools. If Yoshio comes back, I'll see that his tools are all waiting in top-notch condition."

"Will you give it a week, dear," Aunt Ida asked Macy, "before you do something that can't be undone?"

"I'll tell you what," Uncle Emory said when Macy hesitated. "If you still want that doll destroyed by the end of school on Monday, a week from tomorrow, I'll light the bonfire."

"Emory!" Aunt Ida exclaimed.

Macy saw him wink and knew he was telling Aunt Ida, *Macy will change her mind by the end of the week.* She wouldn't, though. The Japs were the enemy, and the enemy had to pay for Hap and Nick. Miss Tokyo was the only one close enough to punish.

She looked at Uncle Emory. "A week. Then a bonfire. A big one."

CHAPTER 34

All through that long week, Miss Tokyo stood near Uncle Emory's shortwave radio in the Farrells' front room. Macy felt the doll watching as she ate her puffed rice, but she refused to imagine the doll's voice in her head.

She took out her journal, but couldn't write in it and put it back.

Uncle Emory began discussing the news with Miss Tokyo. "Your side took a beating at Midway back in June," he told the doll. "Still think you can win this war?"

"She doesn't know about the war," Macy said.

"What, doesn't she listen to the broadcasts?"

"He's teasing, dear," Aunt Ida warned. "Pay him no mind."

"Well, I think that doll's smirking," Uncle Emory said. "She's not convinced yet. Maybe I should turn up the sound."

"She can't smirk," Macy said. "She's just wood."

"Hmm, if you say so." But he turned up the radio anyway. Maybe he wanted to hear it coming in louder.

Macy said in disgust, "She just stands there, dumb and doll-like."

Aunt Ida's eyebrows rose. "Well, dear. She is a doll."

Miss Tokyo was more than a doll, as much as Macy wanted to deny that now. Miss Tokyo had always been more than just a doll, from the day she arrived in this country before Macy was even born. "Papa says she was an ambassador of peace when she came here. When they bombed our ships, I guess her country forgot about that."

"War's a lot more complicated than a doll carrying a message," Uncle Emory said.

Macy dug into her puffed rice. Miss Tokyo wasn't a symbol of peace anymore. She had become a symbol of the Japanese who bombed Pearl Harbor.

Who made Hap become a hero and die. Who torpedoed Nick's ship.

It was all too much. She shoved her bowl away and lowered her head to her arms.

"Wars are brutal," Aunt Ida said quietly. "There's not a doubt in my mind that women and children in Japan and Germany and Italy are grieving for their losses just as we are."

"Monday after school," Macy said, raising her head, refusing to be soothed. "Bonfire. Poof!"

Grief and anger drove her every day. She pushed the rattan buggy through town and collected more tin cans than anyone else, along with fat rendered from meats in people's kitchens and rubber soles from shoes they didn't wear anymore.

She bought defense stamps with every penny that came into her hands. If she saw a war poster coming loose from a nail, she made sure to fasten it back, especially the ones that said *Loose Lips Might Sink Ships*.

Had someone talked at the wrong time, maybe over a shortwave radio, and let the Japanese sub know where Nick's ship was going to be? She used one of her shoes to pound a loose nail harder into a poster.

She tried not to look at the doll still standing in the Farrells' front room, but her heart wrenched the day she saw tears on Miss Tokyo's face. How could a doll cry? She tiptoed closer. The tears were just reflections from raindrops on the window. Macy breathed a sigh of relief. She knew the doll wasn't real. But sadness lay just below her anger. Even cutting out Christmas decorations for the classroom windows didn't help. Snowflakes had nothing to do with the way she felt inside.

Linda and Chris stopped walking to and from school with her. She was too distracted to talk with them. She didn't care. She liked walking alone, and she didn't need Chris saying he was sorry but she had to find out sometime. Or Linda saying matter-of-factly, like they weren't talking about Nick, "My father says when the Japs sink a ship, their subs surface and shoot any survivors."

Macy had walked away, too stricken to say anything. She was vaguely aware of Chris telling Linda she talked too much.

Mr. Oakes walked to the highway with Macy on Thursday, saying he was going up to catch the Greyhound bus to Tillamook and the bookstores. "What do you like to read, Miss Macy? I'll be

happy to pick out a good book for you. Maybe a
funny story to bring back that pretty smile?" He
hesitated. "Call it an early Christmas present."

He was being kind, but she didn't want to
read anything. Christmas this year would be just
another day. She didn't want to be distracted from
collecting scrap and listening to news and pushing
Miss Tokyo's voice from her head. Even the funni-
est book couldn't keep her from remembering her
promise to Mama and Hap to keep Miss Tokyo safe.

She tried not to think of Papa's sorrow. If he
had trusted her enough to tell her about Nick's ship
sinking, they could have grieved together. But he
didn't trust her. He had sent her away. So he had
to feel bad all by himself. And so did she.

On impulse, she startled Mr. Oakes by hugging
him fiercely before turning and running toward
school. He might have been the only good friend
she had left.

Sunday evening as she set dishes around the
table for Aunt Ida, Macy looked over at the doll
and remembered standing beside Mama's chair
while Mama talked of the beautiful pictures in the
book she held open on her lap. She had loved Japan
and its people in a far gentler time. Miss Tokyo and
the book of pictures had linked the two countries in

Mama's mind and heart. As they had in Macy's.

Mama didn't know that Miss Tokyo's people would sink Nick's ship.

"Well." Uncle Emory broke into her thoughts as he came through the front door. "Tomorrow's the big day. Shall I start planning a bonfire?"

"Maybe." Where had that answer come from? A huge hot fire was what she had wanted all week. It was what she wanted for tomorrow. Wasn't it? She couldn't look at Miss Tokyo while she thought about raging flames.

Monday might as well have been a school holiday. Macy sat through every class without hearing anything except the thoughts churning noisily through her own head. The doll had to burn. Japanese sailors had torpedoed Nick's ship. *I'll feel better when I see their doll in flames.*

The image made her shiver. Would she feel better? Could she even watch? The geography book she was supposed to be studying blurred before her eyes.

After school, Chris surprised her by falling into step with her. "I heard about plans for a bonfire. I want you to know, whatever you decide, that's okay with me."

She almost said, *You don't get to choose.* But she had snapped at people all week. Nick and Hap wouldn't approve of the way she had mostly ignored Chris and Linda. Mama would have been disappointed in her, too.

She swallowed her first words and said instead, "Thanks. That means a lot."

The smell of wood smoke reached them before they passed the last of the trees that lined the road from the highway. When they reached the clearing with their two houses, they saw a big bonfire blazing where Uncle Emory usually burned trash.

"Wow," Chris said. "I didn't think he would do that."

He wasn't looking at the fire. He was looking at the rattan baby buggy pulled up nearby. Miss Tokyo stood inside, propped up like a prisoner waiting for execution.

Mr. Oakes called from his front porch. Chris started toward his uncle, but Macy didn't look around. She couldn't move at all. She simply stood on the gravel road, trying to hate Miss Tokyo, trying not to imagine Mama sitting in her wheeled chair beside the buggy, looking sad.

Flames from the bonfire leaped higher as pitch caught in one of the logs. Macy's eyes stung from smoke drifting past. The crackle of burning wood sounded louder and louder. How would it sound while the flames burned the doll?

She should say, *Go ahead. Throw her on there.* But her voice was as frozen as her feet. She couldn't move or speak.

"Macy?" Uncle Emory asked.

She swallowed hard, wondering what had happened to her voice. The smoke, she decided. It stung her eyes and stopped her voice from working. She should step to the side into clearer air.

Miss Tokyo's people torpedoed Nick's ship. She should die for that.

Macy took one step toward the buggy. Then another. She reached for the doll.

CHAPTER 35

Macy!" Chris shouted. "Wait! Uncle Del found a letter. It's for you . . . from your mother!"

"What?" Her voice unfroze. So did her feet. She spun around as Chris ran to her. "A letter from Mama. How could your uncle have a letter from Mama?"

"It must have been in the doll's kimono." Chris held out a yellowing paper folded into a square. "He found it on the closet floor."

Aunt Ida and Uncle Emory came closer. "All this time," Aunt Ida marveled. "You've been carrying a letter from your mother without knowing it was there."

Macy held the folded paper, hardly daring to open it. What if they were wrong? What if it was just packaging to keep the kimono straight? She couldn't stand to have her heart break again.

But Mr. Oakes had said it was a letter. And the paper had a waxy feel, as if Mama had used candle wax to fasten it to the doll beneath her kimono. And there was her name on the front: *Macy*, in Mama's pretty handwriting. Suddenly Macy couldn't wait another moment. She forced herself to open the folds carefully so the old paper didn't tear.

At the top, she saw her name again. Tears filled her eyes. She blinked, trying to make out Mama's writing through the blur.

"*Dearest Macy*,'" she whispered, hearing her mother's voice as she read. She blinked hard, but her eyes kept filling with tears until she couldn't see through them.

"Want me to read it to you?" Chris asked.

Should she trust him? Part of her said no, and she rubbed furiously at her eyes with her sleeve. It didn't help. New tears blurred. She realized that Aunt Ida was waiting for her to decide who should help her read the letter and surprised herself by shoving it toward Chris.

She saw him glance over it before raising his

head to look at her. "Your mom thought war was coming. Listen, this is what she says. *'You found this letter, so you have moved Miss Tokyo. You would not have done that unless she was in danger.'"*

Macy rubbed her coat sleeve over her eyes again. "She still is."

"Here's the part about war coming." Chris read on as if she hadn't spoken. *"'As I write this . . . the Japanese emperor is attempting to expand his empire. I am afraid he will eventually draw our country into war. I fear for the gentle people of Japan whom I knew as a child and who warmly welcomed your father and me when we traveled there after our marriage.'"*

Macy said fiercely, "I told you everyone in Japan doesn't want war. Mama knew that."

Chris had paused several words back. Had he skipped something? She leaned closer and saw that Mama had actually written, *As I write this, my darling . . .*

Boys probably didn't like to read mushy parts.

Almost smiling, she said, "That doesn't sound like Mama. She always added 'honey' or 'sweetheart' or 'my darling.'"

Chris scowled. "You can read that part for yourself. Do you want to hear this or not?"

"I want to hear it."

He watched her for a moment, looking suspicious, before turning back to the letter. "She goes on. *'Even more . . . Macy . . . I fear for you.'*"

He'd substituted her name for something sweeter. Macy couldn't hold back her smile this time. She would learn what Mama had really called her when she read the letter herself.

"*'In wartime,'*" Chris read, "*'passions run high. Remember, although you and I pretended to hold conversations with Miss Tokyo, she is only a doll made of wood with oyster-shell paste to make her face and hands look real. As much as I cherished our game, the doll does not think or feel. She cannot be blamed if war breaks out between our countries. Miss Tokyo has never been alive.'*"

"That's true, you know," Chris said. "You've been getting yourself into a lot of trouble for a piece of carved wood in a kimono."

Papa had said pretty much the same thing, that Miss Tokyo was just a doll, but she was so much more than that. Macy wanted to argue, but she knew it wouldn't change anything.

"Listen to this part," Chris said. "*'I know you will wish to protect Miss Tokyo, and I love you for wanting that. But do not put yourself in danger for the doll. I pray you will take my words to heart. Above all, I wish you safety and happiness always.'"*

Macy felt Chris look at her as if expecting her to agree about the doll not being important. She couldn't, because the doll *was* important. Miss Tokyo represented the people in Japan who wanted to be friends, the people who didn't want war. People here should know about them. When the war ended, friends on both sides would have a lot of work to do.

Chris held the letter out toward Macy. "Look, she added one of those Japanese poems. She says this about it: *'Here is a haiku a friend in Japan sent to me years ago. It was written in 1926 and came in a letter from a girl named Lexie, who sent it with a beautiful Friendship Doll called Emily Grace.*

> *"'Emily Grace glows.*
> *Her warm smile carries friendship.*
> *Sunlight after rain.*

"'The poem's belief in happiness following sorrow has comforted me, as I hope it will comfort you. Remember always to watch for sunlight after rain.'"

He looked up. "And that's it."

Macy leaned nearer to see the closing he hadn't read: *My love forever, Mama.*

"Did you hear that, Miss Tokyo?" she asked softly. "Did you hear Mama's letter?" She leaned into the buggy and pressed her cheek to Miss Tokyo's smooth black hair. "Mama worried about us," she said, her voice sounding shaky. "She guessed war would come and she worried."

Macy stood straighter and tried to think. Mama wanted her to protect the doll. Most of all, Mama wanted her to be careful. Again, she imagined Mama in her wheeled chair beside the buggy, watching the bonfire and looking sad.

"So what's it to be?" Uncle Emory asked. "The bonfire's good and hot. Do we throw the doll on?"

A small sound came from Macy. It sounded like "No."

Tears flooded her eyes again. She wiped them with her sleeve. "No!" It came out louder this time. She grabbed Miss Tokyo and laid her flat in the buggy so she wouldn't fall. In her mind, she saw Mama's gentle smile.

"I know you didn't start the war, Miss Tokyo. And you didn't send that sub after Nick's ship." Her voice broke at the thought of Nick, but she curled an arm protectively across the doll. "I'm so sorry I said all those mean things about you. Mama loved you. I really love you, too."

She turned to look at Aunt Ida. "She's more than a doll. And some little girl posed for her. I just know it. That girl is grown now, and it's like you said that day. She's grieving over the war."

"I'm sure she is." Aunt Ida stroked Macy's hair.

"When the soldiers in Japan crushed all those American dolls," Macy added, "I just know that grown-up girl's heart broke. Maybe she risked her life to hide one of the dolls. Maybe she saved Emily Grace."

Aunt Ida said, "Just as you've saved Miss Tokyo all this time."

"If she did save Emily Grace, she had to go against the soldiers." Macy drew a shaky breath and looked at the big doll with her gentle near-smile. "That was lots more dangerous. All I have to do is say I don't want Miss Tokyo to burn. And . . ." Her voice got stronger because now she was certain. "And I don't."

Mr. Oakes spoke, startling her. She hadn't noticed him come over. "Hiding one of those dolls from Japanese soldiers would be exciting and dangerous, but finding the truth in your own heart can be even harder."

"So," Chris asked, "what are you going to do?"

"I'm going to let in the sunshine." It was almost

funny to see everybody look as if they didn't understand but wouldn't risk asking what she meant. Did they think she would change her mind if they did?

Then Chris said, "You mean like the haiku from your mother's letter. It had that line about sunlight always following rain."

"We're not burning the doll?" Uncle Emory asked.

"No." The word came out strong because she meant it. "Miss Tokyo has to go into storage until the war ends. Maybe she'll have to stay there for a while after that. But someday she'll stand in the museum with all her little lamps and tea sets to show everyday life in Japan again. Boys like Hap when he was little can show their friends that the lamp shades are made of real silk."

She put one hand over the doll. "I want to keep Miss Tokyo so she can share her message about friendship with people who come to see her."

For the first time in more than a week, she let the doll's pretend voice speak silently in her head. *I knew you would save me, Macy-chan.*

I think I knew it, too, Macy answered just as silently.

Somebody was clapping, the sound so loud it startled her. Macy glanced around, but it wasn't

Chris or Uncle Emory and Aunt Ida or even Mr. Oakes clapping. She looked beyond them all to a tall man in blue and shrieked, "Nick!"

Her brother stood near the Farrells' gate, leaning on crutches with Papa nearby, both of them wearing wide grins.

Macy flew across the gravel and hugged Nick so hard she nearly knocked him off his crutches. "Nick! They told me . . . I thought you . . . Oh, Nick! You're alive!"

Laughing, he hugged her while Papa steadied them both. "I didn't hear about all the drama until we got here," Nick said. "Pop told me you didn't know about the ship going down. I wanted to surprise you by just showing up."

Chris came over to stand near Macy. "How come you didn't go down with the ship?"

Macy saw the Farrells looking as if they'd like to tell Chris to shut up, but she wanted to know the answer, too. "This is my friend Chris," she told Nick. "So how come? Why didn't the Jap sub get you?"

"It nearly did." For a moment, Nick's eyes got dark, as if he was thinking of friends who were lost. "I was on deck when the torpedo hit. It knocked me into the water, and I played dead among a lot of stuff blown off the ship."

"Did someone find you?" Macy asked.

"Not right away. I dragged myself into an empty raft and floated for two or three days, then Japanese fishermen took me in. It's a long story. Basically, they patched up my leg and hid me until they could get me to safety."

She hugged her brother again, weak with relief but so happy she couldn't stop smiling. "I'll bet those men had fishing nets held up with rose-colored floats."

He looked at her in surprise. "As a matter of fact they did. How could you know that?"

Macy sighed and leaned against him. "One of those floats got loose, and the currents brought it all the way here to me. Like a message that said you were safe and coming home."

"Sunlight after rain," Chris murmured.

Papa said, "I remember that haiku, your mother's favorite. But I would change it a little. I'd have it say this:

"My sweet Macy glows.
Her warm smile holds forgiveness.
Sunlight after rain."

Macy hugged him fiercely. The war with Japan and the Evil Axis might go on for a long time, but

Nick was home. She felt Mama near, and she didn't feel guilty anymore about loving Miss Tokyo.

Aunt Ida had warned her that Uncle Emory didn't believe in Christmas festivities while our boys were fighting overseas. It didn't matter, even if it turned out to be her second Christmas without a tree. Mama and Hap would be with her in spirit. She knew they would. And with Nick home, she didn't need a decorated tree. This was going to be the best Christmas ever.

AUTHOR'S NOTE

Can an exchange of dolls prevent war? Hope was strong in January of 1927, when American children sent more than twelve thousand dolls to children in Japan. The same hope for peace rose through Japanese children who welcomed the American dolls and helped send fifty-eight thirty-three-inch-tall Dolls of Return Gratitude to the children of America.

Unfortunately, fifteen years later, war broke out. In both countries, the dolls became symbols of the enemy. In America, the Japanese dolls were shoved into storage. In Japan, soldiers were sent to schools to smash the American dolls.

Macy's story in *Dolls of War* is fiction, but the background facts are true. In addition to extensive research, I've called on my own memories.

I was very young when World War II took place. I lived in Rockaway, Oregon, on the northern coast where fear of invasion was real and constant. Whenever we heard the drone of blimp engines, my younger sister and I ran out to watch the huge silvery aircraft fly low over the sea to search for submarines. My family kept a bucket of sand by the front door to put out fires if bombs should fall. Blackout curtains shuttered every window.

Ration stamps became part of shopping. For Christmas and birthdays, we were given savings bonds. Across America, people learned to "make it do or do without." Our country had been attacked, and everyone sacrificed to support the war effort.

World War II ended in 1945. Eventually, the United States and Japan became friends again, but the dolls had been forgotten. Then in the 1970s, surviving dolls were rediscovered. Forty-six of the Japanese dolls sent to America have been recovered from storage, with thirty-eight restored and placed in museums. In Japan, approximately three hundred of the American dolls were saved from destruction and are now on display in schools. (In my writer's heart, I believe that someone brave saved fictional Emily Grace, the doll from *Ship of Dolls* and *Dolls of Hope*, and that she stands among the survivors.)

Shortly after the publication of *Dolls of Hope*, I had the opportunity to fly to Japan and visit Iwasaki Shoten, a company that publishes children's books, including Japanese translations of my series of bear picture books and the Friendship Dolls books. It was a joy to meet Mr. Hiro Iwasaki and his staff and later to tour their beautiful country. It's good to remember that at heart, people are much the same.

For pictures and information on the Friendship Doll Exchange, including current locations of recovered dolls, please visit www.bill-gordon.net/dolls.